THE
GENTLE
DESPERADO

ALSO BY MAX BRAND

Mountain Guns
The Rangeland Avenger
Trouble in Timberline
Three on the Trail
Rogue Mustang
Lawless Land
The Trail to San Triste
The Making of a Gunman
Thunder Moon Strikes
Thunder Moon's Challenge
Gunmen's Feud
Wild Freedom
The Man from the Wilderness
Six-Gun Country
Galloping Danger
Gunfighter's Return
Storm on the Range
Way of the Lawless
Rider of the High Hills
Man from Savage Creek
Shotgun Law
Gunman's Reckoning
Rawhide Justice
The Last Showdown
The Long, Long Trail
The Outlaw of Buffalo Flat
Frontier Feud
War Party
Drifter's Vengeance
Cheyenne Gold
Ambush at Torture Canyon
Trouble Kid
Thunder Moon

THE GENTLE DESPERADO

Max Brand

DODD, MEAD & COMPANY   New York

The Gentle Desperado is comprised of the following stories, which
were originally published in *Western Story Magazine* and written
under the name of George Owen Baxter: "The Gentle Desperado,"
"The Terrible Tenderfoot," and "Tiger, Tiger."

Copyright 1927 by Street & Smith Publications, Inc.
Copyright renewed 1955 by Dorothy Faust
Copyright © 1985 by Judith Faust, Jane F. Easton and
John Frederick Faust

Published by Dodd, Mead & Company, Inc.
79 Madison Avenue, New York, N.Y. 10016
Distributed in Canada by
McClelland and Stewart Limited, Toronto
Manufactured in the United States of America
First Edition

Library of Congress Cataloging in Publication Data

Brand, Max, 1892–1944.
  The gentle desperado.

  (A Silver star western)
  I. Title. II. Series.
PS3511.A87G4 1985   813'.52   85-10321
ISBN 0-396-08715-9

THE
GENTLE
DESPERADO

1

In a little house under the shoulder of a hill lived James Dinsmore, but his favorite dwelling, that in which he had his spiritual being, was a low, round-headed tree on top of the shoulder of the hill. There he could weave a lariat, looking from time to time toward the piled mountains on the one side or the heat mists of the desert on the other; there he could ponder his plans for another prospecting expedition among the higher peaks; and there, also, he could lie on his back and look through the branches at the blue sky or the pure white clouds. There had been a time when he spent more energy and hours on the trail of lost mines than he did dreaming on his hill, but after he turned fifty he began to relax; and thus it was that he was lying on his back looking up through the branches when Robert Fernald came up to him and called out: "Hello, Uncle Jimmy! Here I am!"

Dinsmore started—guiltily, one might have said—and with one hand he combed the disorder, and a few dead leaves, from his magnificent beard; the other hand he extended to greet the boy.

Dinsmore replied to Fernald's announcement of his arrival: "And so you are, Bobbie! And I'm glad to see you! Sit down—wait a minute—lemme see you walk!"

"No," sighed Robert, "I still limp. The doctor says that I always will."

1

"You were a fool kid to ride that mustang," declared Dinsmore. "Sit down here, and tell me about yourself."

Robert sat down obediently upon a rock.

"Lemme see your diploma," said Uncle James.

"I left it below in the house."

"Why, kid, you don't seem very proud of it. Is it everybody around these parts that can sport a college diploma?"

"It doesn't mean much, really," said Robert gloomily. "You don't have to know a lot to skin through a college. But I suppose that law will be different. You have to work in the law school, they say."

"Let the law go for a minute," said the older man in some haste. "But here you are, twenty-two—sixteen years of studying and grinding behind you—and tell me what you have been specially doing with yourself?"

"I was too light for football," said Robert with a greater sigh than before. "I tried pretty hard, but I kept on getting broken up. It seems that I smash rather easily. Too light, and my eyes, you know—"

His voice trailed away. Robert always intended to be stoic, but sometimes he slipped a little.

"Then I went in for boxing," he continued.

"Did you get licked?" asked Dinsmore, rather anxiously.

"Not in my own class," said our hero, setting his jaw in a way that made it seem not quite so soft. "But what good is a lightweight? What good, I ask you? What good in the world?"

His head fell. He prodded at a rock with the toe of his shoe and gouged the leather without stirring the stone.

"You can spoil your shoes, kid," said Dinsmore, "but you can't move a whole porphyry dyke. Well, you didn't do much at boxing, then?"

"Nothing at all!" said our hero.

"What else? Rifle team again, I suppose?"

"Oh, yes."

2

"And pistol team, too?"

"Yes."

"Matter of fact you got a medal or something, I think?"

"You'd laugh to see the shooting we do," said Robert, smiling without mirth. "Perfect guns, perfect ammunition, but men in these days aren't like the men you used to ride the plains with, Uncle Jimmy. They've fallen off a lot!"

"Lemme see," said Dinsmore.

And then he tossed a twenty-five-cent piece a few yards away.

Robert produced a heavy automatic with an easy gesture—as though the gun had been dropped into his hand. And he hardly looked at the twenty-five-cent piece as he said: "Oh, of course, with a target as big and as close as that—"

He fired.

"By jumping Jupiter!" cried Dinsmore.

He leaped up and came back with the blasted coin; one-half of it was blow away.

"Even then, you see," remarked the boy, "I couldn't make a center hit."

Mr. Dinsmore did not seek elegant speech. He said: "Well, what the devil do you want? The world with a fence around it?"

Robert looked up at him and smiled.

"You always want to make me feel that I'm some one," said he. "You always want to make me happy! But I know; I don't forget. You and 'Buffalo Bill' and 'Wild Bill'—why, you could hit a dime at twenty or thirty paces every time!"

"I—" began Mr. Dinsmore, and smoothed his beard with haste.

"I've worked for hours nearly every day," said Robert. "You know—practicing the draw—and snapshots—and yet I can't hit a dime with a quick shot at twenty-five paces! Not more than once in four times, or hardly that."

Dinsmore said nothing. He took out a great black square

of chewing tobacco and bit off a liberal chunk on which he began to work so rapidly that it seemed as though he were eating it.

Robert looked across the heat mists of the distant desert.

He was not seeing the desert, however; he was seeing the future.

"You always knew that I wouldn't make good in this country," said Robert; "but I always hoped that some day, if I worked very hard and patiently, I'd be able to box, and wrestle, and ride, and shoot, and be able to go hunting, and really living, the way you did in the old days. I've studied trailing, for instance, but I haven't the eyes for it. Even these glasses won't completely help. I can't shoot the way real men can. By instinct, you know. And now that I have this bad leg, I can't run all day like an Indian. In fact, of all the things that I wanted most to do and to be, I can't say I've succeeded in a single one. And I see that I'm a failure!"

"How many men can ride or shoot with you, kid?" asked Dinsmore with great heat.

"The world is filled with dubs and fools," said Robert bitterly. "What good is it to be a shade better than most? I'm going to give up the West, and I'm going to settle down to three miserable years in the law school—"

"Hold on, lad," said Uncle Jimmy. "The fact is—I hate to say it—but the real fact is, that the funds have run out. I can't keep on sending you to school!"

"Not to school?" echoed Robert.

Mr. Dinsmore combed his beard vigorously. "Bobbie, the money's all gone," said he, and he looked sadly across the desert and shook his head.

2

When Bobbie saw that the old way was ended and that he was come to the crossroads, he was silent for a moment. Then he murmured: "I didn't suppose—I thought, you know, that father had left me enough. I thought you said so, Uncle Jimmy?"

"Did I?" said Uncle Jimmy, growing rather red. "Fact is, I was always a fool about talk. But you see—I didn't want to have it on your mind. I just wanted you to finish up your college course and—I dipped into my pocket pretty deep to manage the thing."

"That was like you!" cried Robert. "But I want to know what you've spent, and you shall have every penny back that you—"

"Hey, hold on, will you?" said Mr. Dinsmore, growing redder and redder. "It's all right, I say. Don't get excited. But the money used up. Finally—well, some day I'll strike it rich and pay you back everything that—"

"Pay me back what, Uncle Jimmy?"

"Pay you back? What am I sayin'? Bobbie, you ain't accusing me of stealing from you what—"

"Stealing?" Robert exclaimed, his eyes filling with tears—as they often did when he was moved. "Good God, sir, there's nothing under heaven that I trust so much as I trust your honesty and goodness, Uncle Jimmy!"

He clasped the brown hand of the prospector, and Uncle Jimmy muttered: "Didn't mean to have it turn out like this—but there was the money, and it went—not enough left for me, hardly—I mean, not enough left for me to do what I wanted for you! Always considering you, kid, from the first!"

5

"Yes, yes!" said Robert. "And to think that you've been depriving yourself while I idled through college—"

He stopped and mopped his forehead.

"But I'll go to work," went on Robert, "and I'll be able to pay you back before long and—"

"Hold on! Don't run away with yourself. Let the horses do that," replied Uncle Jimmy. "Maybe there's enough left—I mean, maybe I could rake enough together to give you a flying start on that law course and you could raise something from some of your rich friends back East."

"Maybe it's fate," suggested Robert in an awed voice. "Maybe it's fate that has stopped my work in school because perhaps, after all, I could learn to fit into the big things out here in some small way. I don't know what would be the best way to begin. But I think that I should begin by going to the spot where my father lies buried, Uncle Jimmy. A sort of pilgrimage, you understand?"

Uncle Jimmy pointed a brown forefinger at the boy.

"You stick to books!" said he. "Don't you go wasting your training—"

"You don't think that I could do anything real," acquiesced Robert sadly.

"Oh, hang something real!" said Uncle Jimmy. "Is it real to toil in the sun, and get sand down your throat and in your eyes and have sore feet and a sunburned neck, with a danged mustang stumbling under you?"

"You want to make it seem nothing," said Robert, with his wistful smile. "But I've heard the truth from you. I know the wonderful, free, big life that's to be found in the mountains and the desert. The sort of a life that you and Wild Bill—"

"Oh, damn Wild Bill!" said the prospector.

Robert was shocked. Not by the oath but by the name to which it was coupled.

"I suppose," said he sternly, "that no one during Wild Bill's life dared to damn him!"

6

"Oh, well," said Uncle Jimmy, "let's go down and cook a snack for supper. Can you eat pone, kid? Or are you plumb above it?"

They went down to the shack, where Robert made the fire in the crazy cast-iron stove while Uncle Jimmy Dinsmore mixed corn pone and sliced ham. As the ham sizzled on the stove, Robert stood outside the door in the cool of the evening and whistled in a high, weird key, and all the animals of the place came hurrying as to a familiar call.

There was a shambling mule, a lump-headed mustang, a jennet, and a couple of goats which were kept for milk today and meat tomorrow. But tomorrow never seemed to come for them. They gathered about the doorway and from Robert eagerly received various tidbits.

"Now, kid," said Uncle Jimmy after supper, while Robert washed up, "lemme hear what you gonna do with yourself out yonder on that desert."

"I'm going first on a sort of pilgrimage," said Robert, "to the very spot where my dear father—"

"And after you get there?" said Dinsmore.

"I don't know, exactly. I'll find something to do. You know, one must have faith!"

"Faith? In the desert?"

"Oh, yes," said Robert with the quiet of conviction, "because without faith there would be no friendship, or love, or kindness, no trust in the world; there would be no religion, there would be no God in heaven!"

Robert looked up, and a greasy frying pan dripped gray water on his trousers, unregarded.

"Now, look here, and I'm gonna tell you something," said Dinsmore, "and the fact about the desert is that you ain't seen nothin' but the edges and the trimmin's of it. You've gone onto it because it was a lark, and the desert don't pay no attention to kids out havin' their game and their fun. But when you go onto the desert because you have to, then it's likely to be different! It's a treacherous, sneakin', good-for-

7

nothing thing, a desert is. Just when you think you got it patted and petted and smoothed down and sleepy, it just nacherally opens up and swallers you alive. And you never can tell what's stealing up behind to hit you when you ain't looking. No, kid, the desert is like a whole cage full of starved painters. That's how much I would trust it, and nobody with real good sense would ever want to have nothing to do with it at all!"

To doubt his uncle's words never occurred to Robert. But he had already discovered that there were certain contradictory moods and humors in the older man that must be outwardly respected, though they need not be taken to heart too seriously. After a time he said, "But tell me, Uncle Jimmy, why you still get onto the desert whenever you can?"

Mr. Dinsmore gathered his brows.

"The trouble with you youngsters—you all got to argue things. Got to find out for yourselves. Well—"

He left something dire unsaid and fell into a brooding gloom, from which he roused himself only when Robert suggested: "Uncle Jimmy, what about a yarn?"

"I ain't feeling like yarning," declared Dinsmore. "I ain't feeling like making up—remembering, I mean—"

"I'd like to know, though," said young Robert, "about that time you started on the trail of Spotted Antelope—"

"The Comanche? Yep, I remember that and—"

"No, no! The Sioux."

"Well, didn't I say he was a Sioux?" asked Dinsmore, frowning again.

Robert was silent. He could feel the spell beginning to take effect; the atmosphere altered; Uncle Jimmy was donning a robe of dignity and impressiveness, and many an evening in the past had this ceremony been repeated.

"I was sitting with 'Kearsarge' Pete in his lodge, and his squaw had laid some boiled buffalo tongues in front of us. I remember that Kearsarge was feeling kind of mean at her

8

because the day before a cracking thunderstorm blew up and she sacrificed her best dress and a couple of strings of beads to the Sky People to keep a thunderbolt from hitting the tepee. But her and Pete had a kid, and she was kind of soft about it. Pete reached over and picked up a fine pipe and began stuffing it. 'There's a yarn that goes with this pipe,' says he, 'and it takes a back trail to the Sioux; and, by the same token, I'm gonna take that same back trail with my feet and not with my tongue only, one of these days—'"

Softly, moving with utmost precaution lest he make a sound, Robert slipped to his bunk and clasped his hands behind his head. He closed his eyes to the drab little shack and the star or two glinting through the wide edges of the hole up which the chimney passed. The melancholy night wind of the mountains was beginning to sing and brought down from time to time the voice of a wild hunter, the sob of a puma, or the hunger call of a coyote coming out of Bender Pass.

As it was now, so had it been before on how many and many a night!

If he waked, the steady, strong voice of the narrator would continue almost endlessly. And if he slept, what he had heard would pass into reality in his dreams.

Robert's breathing grew more and more regular. Indian ponies, a winter storm, a perilous crossing over an iced river, an avalanche bursting down a mountain slope, the yellow eye of a camp fire looking up from the heart of a black valley—such things passed into his mind with the words of the narrator.

Roused at last from his slumber, he raised his head to see the rose of dawn streaming through the open door. The beauty of the morning and the snoring of Uncle Jimmy filled the cabin with an equal power. He glanced at the open mouth and grizzly, unshaven face of the prospector, and then hurried into the open air.

The grand procession of the mountains assured Bobbie

that all his dreams were true, and he hurried down the slope to take his morning plunge. The pool was sheeted with thin ice along its margin; but if one wants a cold bath, the colder the better; and is he not a fool who quarrels with the provisions of our mother, Nature?

So thought Robert, and with his heel he broke the ice.

3

To Robert it would have been sacrilege to start his pilgrimage after sunrise. Only base, laggard souls will let the sun precede them on their journeys. The sacred enthusiasm sustained Robert even through a breakfast of cold bacon and stale pone, washed down with ice water from the creek, until Uncle Jimmy roused and reared himself upon one elbow.

"You stirrin'?" he asked. "Gonna go fishing?"

He learned then that Robert's instant determination was to start for the grave of his father and thence into the world.

"But maybe you'll find the world before you find the grave," suggested the prospector. "Comanche Corner is a dead town, kid, and it died almost as long ago as your dad. But I'll tell you where it lies."

He took a bit of charred wood and sketched a map on the floor beside his bunk. A chimney butte to the north, and the bed of the vanished river crossing the plain. There he would find Comanche Corner. God knew how many days' ride away; Uncle Jimmy did not!

But what he did know was that he had five hundred

dollars in his wallet and that it must go into the pilgrim's pocket. Robert made stout resistance, but finally submitted because he saw that Dinsmore seemed eager to make the gift, and even heaved a breath of relief when Robert accepted.

So he took the money; clasped the hand of his dear benefactor and guardian; and strode off down the mountainside with a pack on his shoulders, a rough staff in his hand, and a Colt automatic which launched seven shots at one pressure of the trigger in a clip holster under his left armpit.

So had Wild Bill, of deathless memory, worn his weapons when in the prime of his glorious career! And even if a man cannot himself be great, he should follow the best examples.

Robert walked for seven hours that morning. His limp grew worse and worse and his feet sorer and sorer. He began to suffer dreadfully, but tasted joy in enduring this torment; for he felt that he had entered the fire which was to change the metal of his nature and give it the finer and sterner quality which it required. He believed in pain; he believed that it had a purifying property. If that were true, by the time he reached the first village in the foothills, all taint should have been washed from Robert's soul.

He hobbled into the dining room of the hotel and the waitress hooked her thumb over her shoulder.

"Beat it, kid," said she. "No handouts for bums, bindle-stiffs, or tramps royal here. Not in this joint, baby!"

Robert looked upon her in hurt astonishment, but then he saw that she was a woman and that she was young. Therefore she must be good.

He flushed a little, not because of her rudeness but because of his first harsh thought.

"I beg your pardon," said Robert. "I don't blame you for mistaking me for a beggar. I should have brushed my clothes before I came in."

He backed out, and went to find the pump at the back of

11

the building, while the waitress turned toward a man who sat at the long table eating busily. Above his hat mark his hair was brown; below the hat mark it was white with dust, and all the back of his shirt was also white with dust.

"Bud, did you see that nut?"

"Naw, but I heard him," said Bud. "Gimme some coffee, will you?"

Hebe had vanished, however. Presently she was hanging out a back window watching our hero soaking his feet in a bucket of cold water. She saw; she nodded with a knowing air; and without a single question she went to her own room and came down with a strip of cotton cloth, washed and worn to the texture of the softest down.

"Wrap 'em up in this," said she, "and here's some lard to rub on the skinned places."

Fernald looked up to her again and flushed even more crimson than the sunburned tip of his nose. He lifted his hat and said in his timid voice: "You're terribly kind to me! You're terribly kind," he repeated.

"Aw, it's nothing," said she, and vanished to get the coffee for Bud.

But when Robert had struggled into his shoes again—they seemed a size too small by this time—and sat in his turn at the dining table, the girl served him with heaping portions. Twice she lingered near him until he looked up with his wistful smile.

"What made you do it, kid?" she asked.

"I don't understand," said Robert.

"Aw," remarked the waitress, "you been pounding your feet to pulp for nothing, or just fun, maybe?"

"It's foolish to have one's feet give out so soon, isn't it?" he admitted seriously. "But I don't quite understand what—"

"Nothin'! Nothin'!" said she in haste. "I'm a sap. But you never can tell—the birds that come through this town!"

She hurried to the kitchen and came back quietly with a white breast of cold chicken.

"Stow that under your ribs, kid. It'll stick to 'em, I guess."

When he had finished his meal and paid for it, he begged her to accept a dollar for her kindness. Not that it was a reward for her goodness!

She crinkled the bill between thumb and finger; it was real; and she turned from Robert to put the money in a place of security.

He asked if she could tell him where he could buy a horse.

"I can tell you, honey. Everybody in town has got a horse to sell. All crooks! My stars, when you think what a lot of thieves there are when it comes to selling a horse! But I tell you what you do. You go to Hank Chandler at the far end of the town. He's got a little paint horse that'd be a regular sweetheart for you. He'll ask you three hundred. If you pay him more than a hundred and a quarter you *are* dumb! Oh, that's all right." She followed him to the front door. "Is there a 'she' in why you left home? You don't understand? How old are you? Well, never mind! Are you coming back this way again? So long, honey. Now, you take care of yourself. And—hey—you better get a hat with a wider brim or you'll have that nose burned right offn your face!"

Robert, hat in hand, looked earnestly upon the speaker. "I shall never forget you," said he softly. "I never shall forget you!"

The waitress watched him out of sight.

"Aw," said she, "I'm gonna have a heartache for you, baby face!"

Robert walked in a rosy mist, to the farther end of the village. Hank, the horse dealer, sat on the top rail of his corral and talked about the pinto.

Robert heard that this was the one horse that Hank had

learned to love. This was the one horse that his family loved.

"Lord pity me if the missis should ever hear of me sellin' this pony," said Hank, turning up his eyes.

Robert caught his breath.

"I hope that no act of mine—" he began. "I wouldn't wish to be a cause of friction!"

The dealer scratched his chin and looked askance.

"But I see that you got an eye for a horse, my son. And them that knows 'em should have 'em! I'd give that horse away to you for five hundred bucks."

"Isn't that odd?" said Robert. "It's exactly the sum that I have in my wallet!"

He took out the sheaf. The dealer steadied himself on the top rail and added, rather hoarsely: "And I wouldn't mind throwin' in a bridle, kid, at that!"

The money had almost changed hands, when Robert quite suddenly remembered.

"But," said he, "I'm under instructions not to pay more than a hundred and twenty-five dollars for that horse. I'm sorry that I forgot."

The dealer dropped heavily from the fence to his feet. "A hundred and twenty-five damnations!" said he. "Are you kiddin' me?"

Robert drew back a little.

"I'm very sorry," said he. "I don't want to waste your time. I admired the horse so much—but thank you for letting me see—"

He had reached the road when a loud bellow called him back.

"I'll make it two hundred," said the dealer, "and make it even. Doggone me if I'll be able to face the wife though."

Robert hesitated. The voice of the waitress was still in his ear; but, after all, it was only an extra seventy-five dollars. Moreover, Robert knew horses, and the pinto was made like a watch—neatly, and filled with springs, and all his

14

parts fitted together as by the skill of a jeweler. He would never see fifteen hands, and his blood was pure ragamuffin from the plains and the mountain desert, whereas Robert, in his dreams, never mounted anything less than a coal-black charger of at least seventeen hands; but, after all, Robert was himself some ninety pounds short of his wishes and could content himself with a lightweight pony.

He paid the two hundred without more ado. He bought an old saddle, too, and a bridle, and saddlebags, and a slicker. The individual prices seemed small, but the aggregate was oddly large.

"But who told you," asked the horse dealer, eying the little sheaf of bills which our hero was restoring to his wallet at the end of these transactions, "who told you that paint horse ought to go at a hundred and twenty-five?"

"The lady in the hotel," said Robert. "The lady—who waits on the table—"

"That cross-eyed, flat-faced calico!" cried Hank. "I'll teach her to—"

"Don't!" said Robert.

"Don't what?"

"You mustn't, you know. You mustn't speak of a lady in such language."

"I mustn't?"

He roared so loudly that a tremor passed through Robert; and then, looking earnestly upon Hank, he saw that he was in the presence of one of the evil ones of the world.

"Good Lord!" cried Hank. "Are you crowin' at me, kid? A youngster like you! Can't I call that—"

"Not another word!" said Robert firmly.

He raised his hand, his left hand, and shook a warning forefinger. It seemed that Hank was paralyzed with fear. Alas, he was only paralyzed with rage and astonishment. Then, with the flat of his hand, Hank smote the bare cheek of his young customer.

Hank's was a heavy hand, and it shook Robert to the toes; but not so much as he was shaken by another consideration. For in all the frontier tales which had flowed from the lips of Uncle Jimmy, Robert hardly recalled a dozen clenched fists; certainly no blow had ever been struck with the palm! No, in the mountain desert guns blazed instantly when men quarreled, and, as the flames leaped, lives flickered and went out. And he, Robert Fernald, had been deemed worthy of no greater insult than a blow, flatlings, upon the cheek!

Rage turned his hand to steel—that hand which had been ready for the draw—and shooting it up and over from the hip, Bob lodged the knuckles fairly on the point of Hank's chin. It was Robert's favorite punch, in which he had been schooled by the boxing instructor until that gentleman, contented, swore that the blow was as nifty a right hook as ever extracted teeth.

As for Hank, he acknowledged the magic touch by falling on his face like a log; and Robert left him lying there, mounted the pinto and cantered down the street. But even when he was far from the village and the open country received him, Robert's cheek burned hot with shame, as a knight would have blushed who had been smitten with the flat of the sword.

4

Riding was a grateful relief to Robert Fernald after the agony of his last miles afoot, but life on the back of the pinto was by no means perfect. The horse had the beauty of an Arabian, the eye of a lion, and the soul of a mule. He knew all of a mule's tricks: how to arch his back so that his canter bumped the brain of a rider into a dizzy haze; how to stiffen his legs so that his trot racked every bone of him in the saddle; but having gained his point and been allowed to walk, he went swiftly and sweetly, well-nigh as fast as the dogtrot of an ordinary cow pony. But when he felt that a day's march had been completed and that a good camping place had been reached, he was apt to go dead lame. So much so that he could barely hobble on three legs, and exhaustion made him stumble again and again until his dainty nose almost touched the dust of the road. At the first of these compulsory halts, Robert spent an anxious hour massaging the useless legs of Pinto, but no sooner was the little horse turned out to graze than he began to frolic here and there and chase crows with the joy of a reckless boy. So that the first grave doubts entered the mind of Robert, and by the time the third stage of the march was completed he was forced to admit with much sorrow of soul that Pinto was a very knowing and bad-hearted pony.

There is only one way of conquering mulishness, and that is by giving a strong taste of the whip from time to time; and then Robert learned how to smooth the gaits of Pinto, though every time he flogged the horse he sighed with compunction.

The foothills sank behind the pair, turned from brown to blue, and melted at last into the loftier masses of the moun-

17

tains. They were in the desert. Mesquite or greasewood or cactus was the only vegetation, and so scant and so pale was it that it seemed no more than an occasional smoke drift lying low along the ground. When the sun was two feet above the horizon, it had the force of midday heat, and at noon it withered and scorched the very soul. There were dangers for horse and man in this travel, but Robert had charted the water holes in his memory and he was able to knock over a meager, leathery jack rabbit now and again. As for Pinto, if he had the mental traits of the mule he had also the physical toughness of a mule. A good bellyful of water once a day lasted him, or for that matter, he could campaign with one drink in forty-eight hours; for he was of the true desert strain. Break the tougher spikes from the outside of a branch of cactus, and Pinto would devour the rest with neat, small, but patient bites. He was equally patient in gathering grass which had no more substance than streaks of spiderweb. No schooling could teach a horse such desert manners; but a hundred generations of tough ancestry had equipped the mind and the body of the little stallion. Where an ordinary animal would have wasted away, Pinto was growing fat and laughing at the ardors of the journey.

Robert's feet were healing now, and the trip was turning out so much less arduous than he had expected that he began to feel like a conqueror; and like a conqueror he rode into a little desert village which came upon his horizon.

He could see no reason for the town. There was no visible supply of water. The houses were a handful of adobe huts surrounded by no gardens with no touch of greenery. There seemed no more juice of life in the place than in so much dead rock. Barely had he entered the town than he saw a one-armed Mexican beggar seated crosslegged in the full blast of the sun and holding out his hand like a shallow cup, asking alms.

Robert dismounted. Even to a beggar he would not

speak from a height: "Poor man," said he gently, "are you utterly desolate?"

The Mexican rolled up dull, black eyes. He was a pudgy figure, with stomach resting heavily upon his crossed legs.

"Ah, señor," said he, lifting his hat to the questioner, "God gives and God takes away!"

"True," said Robert, with a sigh.

"But one has patience. One endures."

"That is true, also. One endures, if one has courage. I think you are very brave."

"I? I have only the heart which God gave me. No man has more!"

"But how did you lose your arm, my friend? And don't keep your hat off in this sun!"

"It was a little matter of dynamite. We talked, some friends and I. Was dynamite *muy diablo?* A little dry stick, like clay, how could it be *muy diablo?* I offered to hold a stick in my hand while it was set off."

"Good heavens!" cried Robert. "But did your friends allow you to risk your life?"

"No great risk, señor. I held the stick around the corner of a house. However, there was this little accident to the arm. It seemed that dynamite *was*, after all, *muy diablo!* Well, we learn by experience. One cannot be born with all knowledge, señor!"

"And that is true also. Here is a little money. I am not rich or I would make it much more. It will buy you a few meals!" And he gave fifty dollars to the beggar.

The brown-faced man came to his feet with a bound.

"The Holy Virgin watch and bless you, señor! May she be with you like your shadow! May you have ten children, all sons! May your wife never grow old! I, Pedrillo Oñate, foresee that these things shall be. Kind señor, my prayers shall be raised for you every day of my life!"

Robert hurried away. For fifty dollars was not much, and yet it made gratitude run like water from the heart of this

19

poor man, whose loud voice still cried praises and blessings after him:

"May each of your ten sons marry a rich wife, and may the ten wives die young! God give you peace in your old age! May you—"

Robert cantered the pinto around the next corner and breathed more easily when the voice died away behind him. He was flushed, happy. To give is such a joy.

There was a little hotel in this town—two squat huts, joined by a structure of galvanized iron. Bread would have baked in the frightful oven of that dining room.

Robert staggered gasping from the room at last, and went to the stable to watch Pinto finish his rations. Then he groomed the little horse with loving care, saddled him, and started down the street—when behold! seated at the outside, cross-legged, his smoky hand extended for charity, was Pedrillo Oñate!

Robert did not dismount this time.

"Friend," he said a little sternly, "do you not know that there is a point when he who asks for alms becomes a professional beggar? Beware, Pedrillo Oñate, lest some one should apply the term to you!"

"It is my little father!" cried Oñate, unabashed, and smiling up expectantly to Robert. "Ah, kind señor, I thought that I never should see you again except in my dreams. But you are brought back to help the wretched, and aid the poor!"

"Ah?" said Robert, a little staggered by this bland flow of words.

"It never can be said of my little father," said Pedrillo, "that he saw a hungry man—"

"Oñate," said Robert severely, "have you eaten fifty dollars' worth of food and are you still hungry?"

"Alas, señor, I tasted no more than a single glass of beer! I began to think of what I should eat, but it was not fated that I should touch food. There is such a thing as fate, señor!"

"It is true," admitted Robert.

"And fate ruled that I should be robbed of your charity!"

"You have reported to the authorities, then?" asked Robert.

"Would the authorities listen to a poor Mexican? 'Dog of a greaser,' they would say to me, 'out of our sight!'"

Robert began to grow very pale.

"Is is possible that there are such men in this town?" he asked.

"What am I? I am useless. I have only one arm. Why should they consider me? No, they kick me from their paths!"

"Who robbed you?" asked Robert in a trembling voice.

"It is a story, señor," said the beggar. "When I looked down at the fifty dollars which you had given to me, I said to myself: 'It is the will of heaven that Pedrillo Oñate should be made rich this day!' Yes, food for five months lay in my hand. My heart swelled. For five months I could do nothing but pray for my little father! But then I had another thought. It was enough for me, but for my ancient father and my poor mother—alas, even a son with one hand still must think of his honored parents, señor!"

"It is true," conceded Robert. "And I honor you for that thought!"

"Do you, in truth?" said Pedrillo, with a little glitter of insight in his eyes. "Ah, but the poverty of my poor father and my mother! Bent and sick and unable to work! When I thought of them I said: 'You, Pedrillo, may grow fat on this money, but what of your parents?' But everything that the little father has touched is blessed. This money can grow. God will turn it into a great sum. And at that moment I passed the saloon, smelled the cool, fragrant beer, and heard the clinking of the glasses. I went in, and in a back room I saw the gamblers playing blackjack. 'It is the will of God,' said I, 'that I should play in that game!' Hastily I swallowed my beer. I hardly stayed to pay for it. I entered

21

the other room and sat at the table. And just as I had expected, so it proved to be! The blessing of heaven was on the money of my little father! From fifty it turned to a hundred, and from a hundred it turned to two hundred. And all that money I pushed into the center of the table. I was dealing. I won. I was about to take in the big stake— and then suddenly a drawn gun looked into my face. They snatched the money from me. They kicked me from the place. See, señor, where a spur tore my coat! So I must sit here again and beg, and my poor father—my poor mother must—"

Pedrillo began to weep with heavy sobs, but through his fingers he was watching Robert's face.

As for Robert, he thrust his hand inside his coat, but he did not bring forth the wallet. He merely touched the butt of his automatic and made sure that it worked smoothly in its spring clip.

"Now where is the saloon?" he asked.

"It is that fourth house, little father."

"Come there with me," said Robert.

"Little father, what are you about to do? They will beat me if I go in. They will speak lies. They will call me a thief and will kick me—"

Robert turned slowly away. The way of duty lay before him, as clearly seen as any sunlit path. There were three gamblers in that house of dark deeds. And he must oppose them all! But in the olden days, when had Uncle Jimmy turned from facing such odds as these?

When he entered the saloon, three men stood before the bar with little glittering glasses of whisky before them. One of them was speaking, with a chuckle.

"I knew he was as crooked as a snake, but I passed the boys the wink and we lay low and watched him deal. Dog- gone me, Joe, it's a sight to see that one-handed deal and I dunno how he works the cards, but finally—"

"I beg your pardon," said Robert.

They jerked their heads around at him.

"Mr. Pedrillo Oñate," said Robert, "has been robbed of two hundred dollars in this place. I have come to beg you to return his money."

The three looked soberly at him; they looked at one another; they smiled.

"Kid," said one of them, "are you the new sky-pilot? This ain't your church, though! Take the air, boy."

Robert blushed. "Gentlemen," said he, "I do not wish to use force."

"He's drunk," explained one of the three. "Throw the little fool through the door, Charlie, will you?"

"Well," grinned Charlie, "maybe it's my turn."

And he strode toward Robert.

What a thrill of glory passed through Robert at that moment! There could be no question of mere fisticuffs now, for the odds were three to one. He was afraid. He was hideously and shudderingly afraid, but at the same time he had the joyful assurance that he would not be too afraid to fight!

"Friends," cried Robert, "fill your hands!"

Was it not the old time-honored formula? In those words the immortal Wild Bill had addressed his foes before he fired and slew! And, as Robert spoke, he snatched out his automatic with the speed of long and arduous practice. But, for all his speed, he had time to note that the three were not reaching for their guns. He changed his aim from head to hat, blew the sombrero of Charles into the air and sent it sailing the length of the bar.

The bartender dived for shelter; falling bottles crashed like an echo to the booming of the gun; and then the room was still. The three tall men at the bar had gripped the handles of their guns, but they had not drawn.

"Gentlemen," said Robert, "will you kindly take your hands from those guns? Unbuckle your belts, if you please, and let them fall. And remember that I am watching you. My next bullet will be for a head and not for a hat!"

Watch he did, and in tense excitement, waiting for the first twitch of gun from holster. But, to his bewilderment, there was no such movement from any of the three. Pale, silent, with lips compressed, they slowly unbuckled their belts and let them fall, guns and all, to the floor.

It was the only safe way of disarming enemies; Wild Bill had never used any other method.

And now three helpless men stood before Robert.

"Who has the stolen money?" asked Robert.

"What stolen money?" asked Charlie with an oath.

"Don't be a fool, Charlie," said another. "Pass out your wallet. He's got the drop on us. Do the watches go too, kid?"

"Do you consider me a robber?" said Don Roberto, growing very red. "You, if you please—count out two hundred dollars on the bar."

It was done. Two hundred dollars in a stack of rather battered greenbacks lay upon the bar; Robert scooped them up and put them in his pocket.

"Kid," said Charlie, "I don't make out your play, but if you want your name in the paper, this'll get it there! And I'll be immortally danged if you don't get something else besides a headline!"

"Sir," said Robert with the surety of absolute virtue, "I have taken not a penny more than you stole from the helpless Mexican. And if I seem to have taken an unfair advantage of you, you can take up your guns one at a time and we shall settle the matter here and now!"

They were tall men; they were rough men. Their hard hands seemed surely to know every trick of battle and no fear seemed to live in their bright, keen eyes, so Robert waited a moment in breathless suspense. And yet not a move was made! It was odd, but when he saw that nothing more was to be done at the moment, Robert backed to the door, and through it into the street.

The moment the door closed a storm of cursing, shouting, and wrangling began inside the building. He expected to see three fighting men, guns in hands, rush into the street crying for vengeance. No one appeared! The storm seemed confined to the interior of the barroom; so Robert restored the pistol to the clip beneath his left armpit, and went hastily to his horse.

5

Around the corner Robert caught sight of fat Pedrillo Oñate fleeing at full speed, but a shout stopped the Mexican, who turned and threw up his hands as though he expected a bullet the next moment.

Other people were hurrying from their houses, and some of them had caught up a shotgun or rifle as they came. There was no doubt that this little town could prove itself a hornets' nest if it were roused! But the citizens paid no attention to Robert; they looked toward the saloon, from which the shot had been heard and in which the voices now were raging. And Robert felt it was safe enough for him to canter Pinto up to the Mexican.

"Ah, señor, señor!" cried Pedrillo, close to tears. "Did I not tell you that they would drive you out with bullets and with curses? God forgive me for the danger in which you have—"

He paused. Robert was extending to him a hand crammed with paper money.

"They gave me the two hundred dollars which they stole from you," said Robert. "And, after all, it seemed that they were not very violent men."

"San Miguel protect us!" breathed Pedrillo, his black eyes making perfect circles. "One of them is Charlie Bent! Violent men, señor! They will destroy us both! They *gave* you the money?"

Dust had gathered on Robert's glasses. He took them off and wiped them clean, at the same time regarding the Mexican earnestly.

"The fact is," said he, "that they seemed very unwilling to use their guns. After I had shot off the hat of this Charlie Bent, they became extremely reasonable. I think, Pedrillo, you will find that they are men of good hearts after all!"

"Shot off the hat of Charlie Bent!" said Pedrillo, turning pale. "Ah, señor!"

He took the money which was offered to him, and stuffed it into his pocket.

"You have a horse fleeter than the wind, little father," said he. "But what will become of poor Pedrillo? They will shoot me by little bits! Ah, señor, think of me, guard me, protect me! What use is the bone you give a dog if the dog is to be kicked to death for taking it?"

"Come with me, then," said Robert. "I'll protect you if I may. But I don't think there will be any need of protection. You see, they haven't come after me as yet."

"I know them as a man knows fire," said Pedrillo in a voice which quivered with emotion. "Take me with you, kind señor, my master—"

Tears streamed down the brown cheeks of Pedrillo, and Robert was overwhelmed. Pedrillo, with a speed and endurance amazing in a man of his fat, ran from the town; and Robert rode behind him as a sort of rear guard, taking care that they were not followed by danger. There seemed not the slightest chance of this, however, until they topped a rise of ground, heaped up about some stone that broke

26

through the flat face of the desert. Then, glancing back, they saw a cloud of dust sweeping toward them from the village.

"There are seven men!" cried the fat fugitive. "Mother of mercy, fly with me, señor!"

"Perhaps there are seven men," said Robert, his heart beating fast while his eyes strained through the cloud of dust, "but it appears to me that we should not fly, Pedrillo."

"Should not? That we should not? Those men speak with nothing but bullets and they listen to nothing but guns! But if you will ride down that draw, I can show you a way to cover your trail—"

"It begins to appear to me," replied Robert, "that this is a matter which you don't understand. However, if you are afraid because of your wretched life, Pedrillo, take to your heels and run for the draw. I forgive you for the desertion!"

Pedrillo, in fact, ran a little distance, but he turned back again almost at once to the spot where Robert sat his horse, dauntlessly facing the rolling dust cloud that sped across the desert with seven shadows in its midst.

And Pedrillo shouted: "How can I leave you? Señor, little father, are you mad? There are seven!"

"There are seven shots in my gun," said Robert Fernald. "I never should fly except as a matter of strategy. Wild Bill would never—"

The suspicion that there was a little streak of unsoundness in the mind of his patron had no sooner entered the brain of Pedrillo Oñate than he felt that this was the solution of the entire mystery. It explained why the little man had given him fifty dollars, and then had entered a saloon and held up three fighting men at the point of a gun in order to take back the money which Pedrillo's crooked play had won and lost for him most deservedly.

For two reasons Pedrillo hesitated to fly. In the first place, he had conceived a real affection for Robert; in the second, and controlling place, he was by no means sure that he could get away from the townsmen if he trusted merely to his speed of foot.

He decided to play a last card. He fell upon his knees in the dust and caught hold of Robert's stirrup.

"Little father!" cried Pedrillo. "It is well for you to stand and fight against odds. If I were a lone man, a man free from responsibility, I should do the same thing gladly. But I have the burden of a mother and a father who could not keep body and soul together if it were not for me. Fly with me, for three people die in my one wretched body!"

When Robert heard this, he looked down to the shaken form of Pedrillo which stirred in all its fat folds, and then across the plain to the approaching danger. With all his heart he wished to be perfect in his duty; but Pedrillo's argument seemed a weighty one. He turned his horse with a sigh, and presently was riding toward the draw, with Pedrillo holding to one stirrup leather to give wings to his feet.

It was easy to see why Pedrillo had taken the way to this course of a vanished river. The rocky bed would leave little or no trace of the hoof marks, and the sinuous draw was joined at intervals by shallow little steep-walled ravines. Into one of these blind canyons Pedrillo led the way and behind a rocky shoulder Robert dismounted and waited.

Almost at once, they heard the rattling of hoofs down the draw. The hoofs came near, and the noise of the pursuers went past them so close that they could hear a horse stumble in the loose rocks and the loud cursing of a startled rider recovering his seat.

The danger flowed past them, and the noise died away toward the north. At once Pedrillo was all gaiety and mockery.

"Let them sweat on that trail!" said he. "I am fat and I have only one arm, but it is easier to follow the way of a snake in its hole than the way of Pedrillo Oñate across the desert!" Now they left the draw and hurried across the desert to the west. Robert, unwilling that the fat man should wear himself out on foot, offered him his place in the saddle, and Pedrillo, panting, accepted. No sooner was he seated than Pinto pitched him on his head.

Robert lifted the beggar and was happy to find that he was not hurt. He would have had the fat man take the saddle again while he held the bridle and led Pinto, but Pedrillo resolutely refused.

"Better a sprained back than a broken neck!" said he. "A black cloud still floats before my eyes, señor; but it is a wise horse that knows his own master. Moreover, a fool, señor, knows more in his own house than a wise man in the saddle of a stranger."

So he plodded across the desert, promising that before the dark they would reach a good water hole where there would be, moreover, excellent grass for the horse. In the meantime, they scanned the northern horizon but saw no sign of pursuers returning. In good time, as the hot sun rolled down to the rim of the desert, they reached the promised water hole. It was a little oasis of trees, a small area of grass, and a spring which came welling above the sands and running a little distance before it was drunk up by the desert from which it had issued.

"Such are the virtues of bad men," said Pedrillo, turning up his eyes. "They themselves devour their own goodness. Let us camp here. If there is food in your pack, señor, I, Pedrillo, will cook it as food never was cooked before! Ha, look! If there were only a rifle to gather in the rabbit which God gives us for our supper!"

A huge jack rabbit which had been crouching in the roots of a tree near the spring, unable to stand the pressure of fear any longer, had leaped up and fled, dissolved into a gray streak by his speed.

"Rifles are surer, but pistols are quicker, Pedrillo," said Robert, and fired.

A spray of dust stung the belly of the rabbit, which

turned with a frightened squeak as though dodging the teeth of a hound. As it turned, the second bullet struck it and it rolled on the sand.

Pedrillo, momentarily turned to stone, regarded Robert with great, round eyes. Then, without a word, he struck his heel into the sand beside Robert and paced the distance to the rabbit. Here he paused, crossed himself once or twice, and returned thoughtfully.

Pedrillo's meditations kept his voluble tongue silent during all the while he was arranging his fire and preparing the rabbit for cookery, which he did by splitting portions of rabbit meat on long splinters, with bits of smoked bacon interspersed. When he began to turn the spits above the fire, however, and delicious fragrance of roasting meat stole beneath the trees, Pedrillo lifted his earnest eyes to his little father.

"Now it is all revealed to me," said he. "I thought that Señor Bent was a fool to let two hundred dollars go out of his hands, but I see that he was a wise man. I shall respect him more so long as he lives—may the devil take him quickly! Had the rabbit been a man, little father, at thirty paces—"

He stopped, his teeth chattering in his head. And the subject was closed. Still, a change had been wrought in the Mexican's attitude to his companion, and now and again Robert found the dark, keen eyes of Oñate turned upon him as if searching for the solution of a mystery.

The promise of Pedrillo was made good, for never was tougher rabbit made tender; never was such coffee brewed, even in the tent of an Arab. Its perfume delighted no less than its taste, and its power kept joy in the heart long after the few dishes were cleansed and the two reclined in the cool of the evening. They heard the stirring of the wind through the trees; above the far stars shone.

Pedrillo smoked cigarettes of strong Mexican tobacco. Robert lay still and lost himself in a dream. That day he had

30

come to the very brink of a battle to the death and that battle had been undertaken, he felt, in a just cause. Another day, still greater and more perfect, good fortune would come to him.

6

Robert did not waken until the rim of the sun rose above the eastern horizon.

He got up with a sense of guilt that made his heart beat.

"Pedrillo," said he, "I have slept too late. You should have wakened me before—"

Pedrillo did not answer; there was no Pedrillo to answer!

At first, Robert thought that the Mexican had gone hunting for another rabbit with which to break their fast; but when he found that his wallet was also gone, he began to suspect that some other cause was responsible for the disappearance of his companion. And a moment later, when he discovered that his automatic pistol was missing, he knew that the Mexican had drawn the teeth of danger before he fled with his spoils.

For a moment Robert was blinded with bewilderment and rage. After that, he set about finding the trail. There was not a trace within two hundred yards of the camp, but then he came on a spot—as he cut for sign—that showed a trail beginning. And, looking back, he now could see where Pedrillo had turned with the patience and the skill of an Indian and obliterated one mark of his feet before he made another stride.

31

Then Robert saddled Pinto, guessing that the Mexican had not been able to catch the pony. Once mounted on the fiery little stallion, Robert sped down the trail of Oñate like a hawk swooping down the arch of the sky.

Presently Robert came to a point where Pedrillo had taken to a rocky draw such as that in which he sought shelter when the seven were behind them. The natural supposition would be that Pedrillo, once in this covert, would turn away from the direction of the town where his enemies dwelt. For that very reason Robert took the opposite way, for he surmised that the Mexican would double on his course like a hunted fox. Some minutes later he was rewarded by sight of Oñate, trotting steadily down the middle of the hollow.

A thrust of Robert's heels made Pinto leap from the low wall and he landed with a crash at the very heels of Pedrillo, who barely had time to wheel, pistol in hand, when Robert had him by the hair and Robert's knife was at his throat.

In this moment of extreme danger Pedrillo did not attempt a snap shot. Instead, he dropped the automatic and screamed: "Señor—little father—do not stain your hands with murder! It is only poor Pedrillo who means no harm. You kill me already with your terrible look! Ah, señor, spare me! Let me speak! Let me tell you—"

He was on his fat knees, his face gray and congealed with terror. Robert dismounted and picked up the pistol. No sooner was it in his hand than half his fury disappeared.

"Now the money!" said he.

Pedrillo, with a moan, held out the pilfered wallet and the handful of greenbacks which Robert had given to him the day before.

"I want my own, and not yours," said Robert in disgust. "Do you think that I am a thief as you are, Pedrillo Oñate?"

"My life!" cried Oñate, waddling forward on his knees,

and trying to catch Robert's sleeve. "My life, my poor life—my father and my mother, señor! You will not murder me?"

"Murder? I shall take you to the nearest town and the sheriff shall have you!"

"The will of God be done!" said Pedrillo, with a sigh of vast relief. "The will of God be done!"

"What a scoundrel you are!" exclaimed Robert. "To rob me and sneak away. Now try to twist or wriggle away from the manifest truth that you were under some obligation to me; that I had at least done enough to warrant kindness from you, and yet you stole my money and left me in the desert without a gun, and in danger of enemies who had been raised against me by what I had done for your sake. This is the fact. Now let me hear how you will disentangle yourself from these plain truths which damn you as a knave, a hypocrite, and an ingrate, Pedrillo Oñate!"

"Call me a knave, and a hypocrite, and an ingrate," said Pedrillo, "because what virtue is there in me compared with the beautiful soul of my little father—"

"Stand on your feet and talk like a man!" commanded Robert.

"No," said Pedrillo, shaking his head with such violence that the loose flesh of his throat waved back and forth and his cheeks shuddered like twin jellies, "no, little father, I shall not rise until you forgive me, and believe me! I am about to tell you sacred truth."

"Well, tell me what you have to say," said Robert, drawing back a little. At the same time he made a strong effort to banish all his prejudice against this fat, brown fellow. But the effort failed; Robert was a very angry young man. His fingers were tingling with a furious desire to grip the handle of his pistol and—

"Ah, how shall I begin?" wailed Pedrillo.

"With the truth," advised Robert, "because a short, plain truth is better than a whole host of lies!"

33

"With the truth and only with the truth do I deal," said Pedrillo, moving a little nearer on his aching knees. "But alas, alas, little father, this truth is so strange and wonderful and beautiful and strong that even you—"

"Stop it!" said Robert, stamping with impatience.

"Señor, señor," said Pedrillo, shaking his head, "I said to myself that I would waken you and tell you about her. And then I thought that in the morning I would tell you so that you could help her—"

"Who?" asked Robert.

"The Señorita Larkin. I thought of her and her sorrows. Then I told myself that it would be wrong to tell you; you had your own business. It was not my part to take you from your way. Then I said to myself that I myself would go and do what I could, and though it might not be much—"

"What trouble is she in?" asked Robert, more in curiosity than in anger.

"Ah, that I could tell you!" sighed the Mexican. "But no! If you considered in your great heart among what dangers the lady lives, you would turn straight north to the Larkin ranch and you would never stop until you had come to the place, and there you would fight and die for her! No, I never shall tell you how her land is harried and how her cattle are driven away by wicked men. You would go mad if you heard it! But I myself shall go. Only, I remembered that I had little money and no gun. So I took yours, señor, knowing that you would want to use your weapons and your wallet for none but such a good cause as this one. I took them, and I hurried away to get to the place—"

"You should have asked me," said Robert. "I tell you seriously, Pedrillo, that another man would have accused you of robbery!"

"Robbery?" cried Oñate.

"Well," said Robert, "that is what they might call it. But tell me more of the Señorita Larkin."

"But the whole world knows about her," said Pedrillo.

34

"Not I."

"But you have heard of the Larkin Ranch, of course?"

"Never a word before this moment."

"That is a great pity," said Pedrillo. "Once Señor Larkin was like a king in the mountains, his lands were so wide and his cattle were so many. But his rancheria lay in the midst of hills and mountains. The ravines that cut them were so many doors through which the thieves could drive away stolen cattle. In the days of the great Don Gilberto he had ways of fighting men to keep back the trouble a little; but after his death, the robbers had only a woman to fight, and every year her bands of cattle grow less. 'Give up and go away!' say her friends. 'No,' says the señorita. 'Some day a strong and brave man will come to help me, and I shall wait here until he comes!' So still she waits and still—"

"Do you tell me that no one has gone to her help?" Robert asked.

"Ah, yes. They have gone to try, and they have failed! In seven years, seven men have died there."

"This brave woman—her sons have died fighting for her?" asked Robert.

"Sons? Señor, she is only a girl! She has not twenty years, I think."

"Dear heaven!" murmured Robert. "Is it possible that a woman could be such a child and still so brave?"

"She is her father's daughter."

"God forgive all men!" sighed Robert. "And such a wonderful and beautiful woman is allowed—did you say that she was beautiful, Pedrillo?"

"Beautiful? Alas, señor, if I were to talk of her, you would say that even your poor servant, Oñate, is a fool and a boy! Her eyes—"

"No, no!" said Robert. "I would not go to serve her simply for the sake of her beauty, but only because she is a woman and in trouble. Tell me, Pedrillo—no, first stand up!"

35

"You forgive me, señor?"

"Forgive you? For what, my poor friend?"

"Because I dared to take—"

"My money? My gun? But only to give them to a woman who needs them? Pedrillo, I not only forgive you, but I should despise you if you had done any other thing. You have taught me my duty!"

"I? I could not!"

"Hush! Tell me in what direction we should go?"

"North, north, señor. North, of course, in the very direction that I was traveling! But consider that there is a terrible danger—"

"We must not be cowards," said Robert, "dying in fear whenever duty beckons to us."

"But there is Lefty Tom Gill, leading those manslayers, those—"

"Lefty Tom Gill!" cried Robert. "Is it the man who raided Black Gulch and shot the sheriff of—"

"Aye, señor. But he is older now, and therefore he is more terrible; and his men are chosen from among the worst of all the—"

"Let them be chosen where they will,"said Robert, "I have heard of this man before. He was a scoundrel in the days when my father still was living. He has been a scoundrel ever since. If I can destroy him, I shall be doing a work that my father would have been glad to do had he lived a little longer! I thank God, Pedrillo, who sent you to me to show me what to do!"

Pedrillo, having rubbed some of the pain out of his knees, which had been grinding on the hard rocks until they were a torment to him, now mopped his streaming face. He seemed to have grown older. His flesh hung in folds. Only by degrees did he regain his former assurance and his normal red-dashed color. Still he regarded his reconciled master from the side with an odd mixture of contempt, terror, and astonishment. He measured the dis-

36

tance between them and the hills as though considering that many things could happen before they reached that goal, and then he cried heartily: "Señor, we waste time. Let us go forward!"

"True! True, Pedrillo!" replied Robert. "Let us go forward! But tell me—is it not strange that from the beginning of time women in great distress—even in the most ancient books, Pedrillo—is it not strange that always they are beautiful?"

7

Such was the beginning of Robert's venture against the cattle rustlers who preyed upon the Larkin Ranch, and all other ranches in the broken range which fenced the desert to the north. The way was long, but the cunning of Oñate took them to every water hole with an unerring instinct as true as that of a wild horse, and the purpose of Robert was not dimmed in its strength and its luster.

So they came to the mountain wall, and as they labored slowly up the incline, he began to appreciate the superior mountaincraft of Pedrillo. For the canyons on either side came to blind walls over which the water poured in a crashing white torrent, and there was no thoroughfare for any creature unequipped with wings. The spur made hard going, but by means of it they wound slowly but securely through the belts of greasewood and cactus; and then through a region of stunted shrubbery, and so up to a level of lofty pines, which closed high above their heads.

While they were still in this region they came to a summit from which Robert had his first view of the Larkin Ranch. It was in a great bowl with an uneven, rolling bottom, edged by the ragged and deeply bitten ranges of hills and mountains. He could hardly guess at the thousands of acres of grazing land which it comprised, but he knew that the sparkling streams of water and the growth of fresh green grass must make an ideal pasturage. He could see, too, that this was a paradise for cattle thieves, for out of the dark mouth of any canyon that split the mountain rim they could swoop down on a scattered group of cows, and drive them away in comparative security.

There was not one such canyon, or two; but a dozen shadowy recesses opened among the heights.

"There are two things which could be done," said Robert at length. "Either the canyons must be blocked—which is impossible—or else such strength must be here in the valley that cattle rustlers will fear to come down more than they fear riding into fire."

"Aye, señor," said the Mexican. "If that could be done—"

And he smiled covertly and looked straight before him, not daring to turn to Robert lest the latter should see the mockery in his eyes.

They came in sight of the ranch house late that afternoon. A noble cluster of trees stood around it, and it extended two large, comfortable wings like welcoming arms. It had grown by fits and starts, according to the whims of the rich rancher who had planned it. The great stables, sheds, and barns lay well away from the house, and the fields through which the two travelers rode were liberally dotted with cattle.

"Surely," said Robert, growing more and more thoughtful, "the owner of all this land and cattle is rich and untroubled!"

"So one would say, señor," said the Mexican, "but often as great men grow they carry a growing mortgage with them. So it is here, and the whole world knows that the señorita loses money every year and the banks will not help her any longer."

"Business is a mysterious thing," said Robert seriously. "I have tried to understand it before, but I have given up. We must go faster, Pedrillo! I long to see the lady!"

Pedrillo, it must be admitted, was a matchless pedestrian. He could not walk fast, but he never stopped, and though he perspired incessantly, his shadow never grew less.

In the evening they came to the ranch house through the cool cloud of trees that surrounded it, and found Miss Beatrice Larkin walking up and down the long veranda which wound about the irregular front of her house. A tall, spare youth walked beside her. Near the front door an elderly lady looked up from her knitting, from time to time, to watch the growth of the evening shadows dancing among the trees.

"It is the sister of the mother of the señorita," said Pedrillo, whose eyes were growing round with awe as they approached the mansion.

Robert dismounted and stood at the foot of the steps. Miss Larkin paused with her companion just above him. She was a brown-faced girl, dark from constant exposure to the sun which had faded her hair from brown to almost a straw color. She was small and slender, but a great spirit found expression in her keen eyes and restless gestures. At a little distance it had seemed to Robert that she walked and talked like a man; but when he came closer and saw that Pedrillo had not overpraised her, he lost the power of speech.

"Hello!" said Miss Larkin. "Where did you blow in from, stranger?"

Robert merely stared.

"Well, sonny," said Miss Larkin, "what's wrong?"

A lump in Robert's throat was seriously in the way of his

speech but he managed to stammer that he had come from the direction of the desert.

Miss Larkin smiled. Or rather, she grinned, for there was something boyish in her expression.

"I didn't think you came from the mountains—and Tom Gill," said she.

That gave Robert a perfect starting point, and he said: "I've come about Tom Gill, Miss Larkin. For I hear that you need help—"

"Help? I need an army!" said the girl. "Hold on! Are you Sheriff Matthews' boy?"

"No. My name is Robert Fernald. I have no help to offer except that of my two hands, you see."

He spoke with gravity and modesty. Miss Larkin looked keenly and quickly into the fresh face.

"You came to fight Tom Gill. Is that it?" she asked crisply.

"Yes," said Robert.

Miss Larkin stared. She raised her eyes, and saw Pedrillo in the background, significantly touching his forehead; then she said quickly: "It's mighty fine of you. Tumble your pack off that horse and—Martha! Martha!"

A voice echoed from the interior of the house and footsteps approached down the hall.

"Show Mr. Fernald to a room. We'll have a talk after dinner."

In two minutes Robert was safely out of sight, and sitting rather stunned, in a large, cool, clean room. He felt, somehow, that his entrance had not been very impressive; but at least he was on the ground and afterward he would find his chance for action. In the meantime, there was Beatrice Larkin. He wished that her voice were a little softer, her step a little less briskly swinging, and her eye less commanding. Nevertheless, in spite of these faults—or perhaps even partly on account of them—she filled his mental horizon.

He barely had time to make himself clean and neat—and look to the condition of his automatic—when he was called

40

to dinner. It took a good deal of effort on his part to answer that call, but when he got downstairs, the atmosphere had changed. He was received with gentleness, almost with pity, he thought. And now and again he was vaguely aware of glances meeting behind his back. But all was kindness and hospitality, and Robert was soon quite at home. The only disagreeable feature was the presence of the ranch foreman, who was introduced as Dan Parker. He took Robert's hand in a grip of iron and looked keenly, quizzically into his eyes. That grip and that stare kept Robert a little flushed for several minutes, but during the rest of the meal, Dan Parker's head was bowed between his mighty shoulders and he attended exclusively to his food. Miss Larkin was absent-minded and silent, also. Her youthful companion, Fitzroy King, who seemed to be a guest, ventured a remark now and again, but got short answers from Miss Larkin. Only the aunt, Miss Harriet Atkinson, maintained the conversation in a quiet, pleasant voice.

After dinner Miss Atkinson talked for a time with Robert—about himself. He explained to her a few of his ideas. And he told her that he really did not hope to rival Wild Bill, or any others among the truly great; only he hoped that he would be able to do something in a small way. And if he could but meet Tom Gill—

Miss Atkinson listened with wonderful sympathy and understanding; she was sure that her niece was grateful for his help. And perhaps, indeed, he might be the means of lifting the terrible cloud which hung over the ranch.

Robert said good night and went to bed. But after he had passed the door—which was framed with a crack so ample that voices passed easily through it—he heart Miss Atkinson say: "A terribly pathetic case, my dear!"

And he heard Miss Larkin answer: "Sad or crazy. I don't know which!"

Robert wondered what they were talking about, but he was too sleepy to think things out.

The desert fatigue had left him when the sun rose, and

he went downstairs where he met Beatrice Larkin singing as she hurried toward the front door, clad for the day's riding on the range.

"If I may have just a little minute of your time, Miss Larkin," said he, "I'd like to know what you could suggest for me to—"

She hardly turned; she merely waved a hand and said vaguely: "Just rest up for a few days, Mr. Fernald!" She was gone, the screen door banging loudly behind her.

So Robert went out, feeling rather dazed and downhearted, and found Pedrillo. Pedrillo was in the best of spirits. He had found a blackjack game in the bunk house and his capital had increased in consequence. After talking with Pedrillo, it seemed best to Robert that they should ride the range themselves, drifting far toward the northern mountains. One could not tell when they might come on traces of terrible Tom Gill and his men!

Pedrillo got a broncho; young Robert's armament was increased by a borrowed rifle; and they rode out on the plains. By supper time they returned with nothing gained except a closer knowledge of the land. And so it was the next day and the next. But when Robert came in on the third night, Dan Parker met him.

"There was three hard-boiled gents blew in and said they was looking for you," he declared. "I said that they wasn't. They said that they was, and they described you pretty close—you and the Mexican. But I give them the run off the place. Only I got to tell you, sonny, that if any of them three meet up with you—they'll eat you raw, because they're pretty mad. And I'll tell you one more thing. All the time that you're on this here place, I'm watching you, kid, because I don't take nothing for granted!"

As he said this, he tapped Robert's chest with a finger like a rod of iron.

It was very uncomfortable, and the worst of it was that it seemed to leave Robert nothing to say. So he went into the house for supper and that night it occurred to him that his

42

hostess was more than a little weary of his presence. Or was it only that her mind was too much occupied with her own troubles?

For she said at table—where the talk had been rather listless: "If Sheriff Matthews doesn't bring a hundred men and comb those mountains, I'll let the world know that he's a quitter and a coward!"

It was a brief explosion, but it made Robert tinglingly glad that he was not Sheriff Matthews.

So, next morning, he rose with an iron determination to accomplish some definite thing. And, first of all, he hunted out Pedrillo.

"Pedrillo Oñate," said he, "we're starting for Tom Gill again today. But we're going to change things around. Suppose that you were Tom Gill. Suppose you were raiding this ranch. What would you do? Think it out that way, Pedrillo!"

"Ah, señor," said Pedrillo, "but suppose that I should think right—and suppose—God forbid!—that we should meet Tom Gill!"

"Ah?" cried Robert. "And what under heaven has brought us here, Pedrillo? What was the noble motive that made you—"

"Alas, señor," sighed Pedrillo, "noble motives will not stop lead bullets!"

"I understand you," said Robert scornfully. "But even if your first fine purpose is growing weak, Pedrillo, we must keep on, for I have taken an oath that I never shall leave this trail until I find Tom Gill! God is my witness!"

He raised his face and his right hand to the sky—and was well-nigh blinded by the sun.

Pedrillo did not laugh; he was still lost in gloom as they rode across the hills toward the mountains. It was mid-morning before they reached the base of the mountains, and they rested in the saddles, watching two riders drive three or four hundred cows ahead of them.

"We must go to the mountains and live there and hunt

there," said Robert. "We never shall find Tom Gill on the plains! They make their raids by night, and by day Miss Larkin's men ride everywhere. See, there are two of them even here at the edge of the range!"

"But it is a strange thing, señor," said Pedrillo, "that Miss Larkin's punchers should be driving the cows toward the mountains. And look, señor! They are taking the cows at a trot!"

So it was, indeed. Why should they be driving those cows in that direction?

"We'll ride up and ask," said Robert.

"My horse is lame, señor!" cried Pedrillo.

Robert turned quickly in the saddle and saw the sickly yellow-greenish color of his companion's face.

"Pedrillo, you coward!" he cried. "You act as though Gill were riding there!"

"The Virgin of Mercy shield us!" moaned Pedrillo. "But if that is not the gray horse which no man but Tom Gill rides—"

"It could not be!" said Robert, trembling, but trembling not with fear alone. And the next instant a whip cut on Pinto's flank and sent him bounding forward.

Indeed, it did not take long to tell that these were strange cowpunchers, for when they saw they were approached from the rear, they dashed at the cows, hurried them into a gallop toward the mountain pass which gaped just before them, and then drew from holsters beneath their legs long rifles which flashed brightly in the sun.

So Robert knew, with an excitement that almost stunned him, that whether or not yonder rider on the gray horse were Tom Gill, here were two thieves working in the broad light of day.

He looked back. Pedrillo was following, indeed, but following only at a hand canter and sitting stiff in his saddle; rather like an observer than one bent on mischief. And that left two men on Robert's hands. If one of them were Tom Gill, then he was lost, to be sure. But he could not turn back. It seemed to Robert that the ghost of pretty Beatrice Larkin drifted somewhere behind him, an armed ghost, rushing fiercely after these robbers. It was a wild illusion, of course. But it made it impossible for Robert to turn his horse, in spite of his fear.

His was a real terror. Now he realized clearly that he had been on a fool's errand, seeing that Tom Gill was one of those very immortals about whom Uncle Jimmy had spoken so often. He prayed that Tom Gill might not be one of the two riders, and at the same time he stopped whipping Pinto forward. There was no need of whipping, however. The little stallion loved a race as well as any creature in the world; and now he had taken it into his heart that this was a race against yonder two riders, and he was giving his best, stretching lower and longer as he increased his stride, and fairly winging his way over the rough ground. Perhaps that longer striding pair could have distanced him on level going, but not over this sort of running. Besides, they seemed to have no intention of merely bolting. They kept the cows at a gallop, headed for the pass, and now one of them turned in the saddle and pointed his rifle—

For the first time in his life, Robert heard a bullet rip through the air above him—a bullet intended for his own body. And what a difference that made in the sound! He ducked lower; he flattened himself against Pinto's neck. If only the little mustang would go slower! No, Pinto raced on, gloriously, madly, his ears flattened with his effort. And every instant they drove closer to the formidable pair. Robert's thought changed. Let him be struck, if struck he must be, in leg or arm, a wound which would topple him from the back of his horse!

Two more bullets sang past him. They missed, and Robert groaned to himself: "They're just warning me away! And when they make up their minds, I'm done for!"

Only a mighty sense of shame kept him from reining in Pinto as the little horse streaked across the rolling ground. It all seemed part of a trick of fate, now, that had put him on the back of the mustang so that the horse could, in the end, dash him to his death!

Then something nipped his cheek; that side of his face became numb; there was no pain, but hot blood began to pour down.

He had been hit! He touched his face with his hand and it came away dripping and crimsoned. Surely, now it was time for him to turn back. He had been struck with a bullet. Now even Miss Larkin would take him more seriously. He pulled at the reins!

But Pinto had the bit securely in his teeth and he minded that pull on the reins not a whit, except to shake his head and then stretch it forward.

"I'm lost!" thought Robert.

He saw the two before him bring their horses to a slow canter, and swing around, with rifles poised.

In desperation he whipped out his own rifle and took a snap shot at the man on the gray charger.

He did not stir from his saddle, but yonder—behold!— the second man had doubled over and dropped his rifle to the ground with a yell that rang far and faint in the ears of Robert. He had shot his first man! Ah, not fatally, thank

God! For the fellow had swung to the right, was lying low along the neck of his horse, and was fleeing for his life.

That was not all, for when the man on the gray horse saw what had happened, he pitched forward low on the neck of his mount, and drove to the left into some scattered trees!

It was not Tom Gill, then, for Tom Gill would never turn his back on any man or group of men. It was not Tom Gill; therefore, why might not Robert overtake this rider and fight him to a finish with a chance of victory? The first success had filled him with the same glorious madness that possessed Pinto, and the next moment he was rushing through the trees of that open copse. Again and again Robert had glimpses of the fugitive, once so near that he could see the strained and desperate expression of a broad-faced man, grizzled with middle age.

Robert thrust the rifle back into the sheath and snatched out the automatic, for when he next had sight of this man, it would be a close thing. The gun was hardly in his hand when he had a nearer view of the flying horseman. He fired, and in answer the pursued swung his gray around and fired point-blank.

The bullet twitched at Robert's coat as it tore through beneath his armpit. As he felt the jerk he instinctively fired in reply, hardly so much as pointing his own weapon.

The rider of the gray lurched from the saddle and lay on the ground face up, his arms thrown wide! A moment later, while Pinto touched noses with the tall gray, Robert knelt by the motionless body, and saw a red streak across the forehead of the fallen man.

Death, surely!

In the quiet that followed the firing, Robert felt that the tall, dark trees were watching and listening, and he was half frightened by the heavy breathing of the horses, and the creaking of the girths as their bodies heaved.

It was as if a ghost had voice when the fallen man

47

groaned. Yes, groaned, stirred, and sat up with his hand pressed to his head!

"Thank God!" said Robert. "I thought you were a dead man!"

"It's a kid!" said the other with a snarl. "A pink-an'-white kid! Ten million damnations! Nobody'll believe it! Chuck done for—and me!"

"You're bleeding still," said Robert politely. "Will you let me tie up the wound?"

"Aw, go to hell!" answered the unromantic cattle rustler. "I ain't hurt. I ain't hardly scratched! If I'd bore a bit to the left, I'd of got you clean, my fine young bird, eh?"

And he pointed to Robert's wound.

It was an excellent remedy for the boy's sentimentality. It enabled him to order his prisoner crisply to his feet; it enabled him to tie the man's hands behind him and make him climb upon the gray.

"Everybody'll know there was something wrong!" said the prisoner. "They'll know that a baby-faced brat like you never could have beat Tom Gill in a fair fight!"

"*Tom Gill!*" cried Robert. "Did you say that your name is Tom Gill?"

"You blockhead!" answered Mr. Gill. "Who else in these parts rides Lucky Joe, will you tell me?"

Robert could not answer. Awe, wonder, and a peculiar shame possessed him. For, after all, what Mr. Gill said was perfectly true; and if luck had brought his rifle bullet a little more toward the center, there would have been a dead Robert Fernald—dead with a bullet through his brain!

Shame-faced, dizzy, and unable to realize what had happened, Robert rode out of the woods with his prisoner, and met Pedrillo riding slowly up.

When he saw this tableau, the Mexican went almost mad with joy. He threw up his one hand. He swayed in the saddle. He crooned in hysterical joy.

"Señor, my master, my dear brother!" cried Pedrillo.

"We have won! Together we defeated them! Ah, Señor Fernald, we are famous men."

He continued in this vein for some time, meanwhile tying up the wound in Robert's cheek, which he pronounced no more than a little scratch.

"I only got one thing to ask of you, kid," said the rustler, at length.

"Whatever I can do, I shall," said Robert willingly.

"Then shut the trap of this fool, will you?" asked Tom Gill. "Because hearin' him yap sort of tires me a little. I have et greasers," he added to the Mexican. "I have had 'em for breakfast and for lunch. I have most likely used your pa and uncles and your brothers for targets, you yaller-faced, cross-eyed, one-handed streak of nothin'!"

"Dog of a thief and sneak and coward!" cried Pedrillo. "You know that your hands are tied and that I cannot strike you, or I would shoot you to—"

"Be quiet, Pedrillo," said Robert. "Go back and head the cattle from the pass!"

"It ain't any use, kid," said Tom Gill calmly. "Fact is, none of the boys'll have the heart to bother them cows after they hear that I've had a piece of bad luck! They've damned me and hated me and spited me, but now that they ain't got me to lead 'em and show 'em what to do, why, they ain't gonna be so brisk! About the whole gang of 'em is gonna slide before morning, I take it! They'll see who was the man of the party!"

Tom Gill made this speech with a sort of sneering self-satisfaction, and rather to himself than to Robert, whose opinion of his famous prisoner was sinking mightily with every moment that he listened. Suddenly Gill said: "What name did the Mexican call you, kid?"

"Fernald."

"Well, I knew a Fernald in the old days."

"You did?" said Robert coldly.

"But he was a hard-boiled one," went on Tom Gill, "and

no kin of yours. There was only one amusin' thing he done, that low-down murderin' hound. And that was to cuss. Doggone me if he wasn't a corker at that! I seen him lay dyin'. I wish that it had been my luck to sink the bullet in him that stopped him! But even when he was croakin', with his head in Jimmy Dinsmore's lap, dang me if his cussing wasn't a thing to listen to and remember! Only it was too fast to memorize! But I'll be darned if he didn't leave sixty thousand cold iron men, that four-flusher. He'd hit it rich!"

Rage had been slowly gathering in Robert's breast, but rage was displaced by astonishment when he heard this last statement. Mathematics never had been a favorite study with him, but he knew enough to understand that sixty thousand dollars at six per cent makes thirty-six hundred a year. And the bitter truth was that Uncle Jimmy Dinsmore had never spent half that sum upon him in any year. How, then, could the fortune have been dissipated?

"Sixty thousand!" breathed Robert.

"It sounds much, kid, don't it?" remarked Tom Gill. "But Fernald left it to a windy old crook named Dinsmore. The outlyin'est man that ever spun a yarn. We used to like to hear Jimmy talk so's we could laugh, afterwards. By his fireside he must've killed a hundred men or so. Always talkin' about Wild Bill, that must've died while Jimmy was in short pants. Well, Jimmy must've had a real gay time blowin' in that wad of money. He had a flyin' start right there in the camp. And I'm kind of glad of it, because a four-flusher like Fernald didn't deserve—"

"Mr. Gill," said Robert coldly, "you're speaking of my father!"

Gill gaped, bit his lip, and then was silent.

When he spoke, it was in a humble tone: "If I had knowed, kid," said he, "I wouldn't have yapped like that. But you ain't got the look of your dad, y'understand? I couldn't guess."

Robert, white with anger and grief, said nothing, and

Tom Gill added after a moment: "Me and your dad never hit it off. You put down some of my talk just to hard feelin', will you?"

"And the sixty thousand dollars?" added Robert with a burst of hope that Uncle Jimmy might have been slandered.

"Aw, I seen that paid over in dust and nuggets. I seen it weighed out with my own eyes. So did a hundred gents besides me!"

Robert's cheek began to swell, pressing hard against the bandage. The pain, the loss of blood, the burning heat of the sun beneath which they were riding raised a fever. He began to breathe hard, to wish that the miles to the ranch would quickly disappear. They dragged on, however, with a mortal slowness. In a semi-delirium Robert rehearsed what he had heard. His ideal picture of his father, if not destroyed, was at least tarnished sadly. The admiration with which he regarded Uncle Jimmy Dinsmore now seemed to have been paid to the worst of scoundrels, who would steal from a helpless child! He shook his head, but he could recall now, some of the words of Uncle Jimmy—words which that wily man had uttered at their last interview. And Gill's statement seemed gloomily substantiated.

So that morning wore away and deep into the hot afternoon they rode. The Mexican, after lingering with them for a time, had raised a surprising burst of speed and dashed away across the hills in the direction of the ranch house.

"Look at him!" grinned Tom Gill. "The rat'll get in there and hog all the credit before you arrive, kid. But I'll sink his ship for him! I'm gonna let the world know the truth, just to spite their eyes! It was you—and luck—that downed me! Aye, come foamin' and shoutin', all of you! You none of you had nothin' to do with this here!"

51

Robert knew what a triumph was like in the days of ancient Rome. It made him very happy to have these rough men surge around him, clap him on the back, hope that his wound was not serious; shake his hand, and tell him that he was "all right!" With conviction they said it, and being men of few words their praise had weight and meaning. They laughed at the pride and conceit of Pedrillo, but they laughed with the utmost good nature. "The Mexican thinks this is his day," said Dan Parker. "Let him crow a while!"

Robert was very happy, but he was ashamed, too. They were making too much of what he had done, and he felt a rising sense of guilt; particularly when they reached the house and young Fitzroy King shook his hand and congratulated him; but even more than that when he was alone with Beatrice Larkin and her aunt. Miss Atkinson was extremely gay; she looked upon Robert with affectionate eyes and had an air of one who "told you so."

Robert could stand no more. He became more and more depressed, and finally cried out: "I can't let you go on like this. It—it isn't right!"

For Beatrice Larkin had said: "I think it's going to mean everything to us. We're going to keep the place together. And that means my father can rest happy in his grave." She said it with tears in her eyes. And now, as he protested, she looked at him with a touch of horror.

"Why isn't it right, my dear boy?" asked Miss Atkinson.

"Because," said Robert, "you make me out a hero, and I'm not. I was—afraid all the time!"

He brought it out with a mighty effort, his hands clenched.

"And when I saw Pinto overtaking them, I would have turned back; but he had the bit in his teeth. I couldn't stop him; he just thought it was a race! I—well, I was desperate. I fired at Tom Gill—and the bullet hit Chuck and made him gallop away. Then when I saw Tom ride to escape from me, of course that gave me more courage. I didn't dream that it was Gill or I never should have dared to go after him. I rushed Pinto into the woods and by a lucky shot managed to knock Gill out of the saddle. When I found out his name afterward—why, it just about paralyzed me. I wanted to be what you thought I was. But—I had to tell the truth!"

He could not raise his eyes as he heard the cold, clear voice of Beatrice: "It seems that Pinto was the hero, and not his rider!"

"Yes," said Robert. "It was Pinto!"

"Humph!" said Beatrice, and Robert shuddered.

"It doesn't seem possible," said Miss Atkinson in a wavering voice, "that there really can be any one like this." She came to Robert and took his face between her withered hands and made him look up. He was amazed to see tears trickling down from her eyes. "It *is* possible!" said Miss Atkinson. "You—you—"

Miss Atkinson hurried from the room, and as she closed the door Robert heard her sob.

He stood up, shaken.

"I'm sorry that—that I upset her so. I think that I'd better leave right away, Miss Larkin. Thank you for putting me up."

He got to the door, but there he was caught by the arm and drawn firmly back.

"You inconceivable little idiot!" said Beatrice Larkin. "Don't you see it was because poor Aunt Harriet was overcome by your modesty. I even am myself, a little! Don't you understand? You haven't done any shameful thing.

53

You've been a hero. You've done the greatest thing that's ever been done in this range of mountains since God raised 'em out of the sea. Go upstairs and lie down and I'm coming along to dress that wound in your cheek for you!"

Robert obeyed as one in a dream, and yet it was such a happy dream as it is given to few to enjoy.

When Miss Larkin came, she found Robert delirious, with an alarmingly high fever. She called in Miss Atkinson, and together they ministered to him.

The two women discovered that if Miss Larkin remained in the room the sufferer was quiet and slept; but if she left, he grew swiftly and astonishingly worse.

"I don't know what it means," said Beatrice Larkin, frowning.

"You dishonest little minx!" said Miss Atkinson. "It means that another poor man has fallen in love with you. You know it better than I do."

"I suppose I do," said Miss Larkin, "the poor baby!"

"Baby? Hero!" said Miss Atkinson.

"Baby!" insisted Beatrice, and she patted Robert's hand.

In the middle of the night Robert wakened from a frightful dream and started up terrified, until by the lamplight he saw that Beatrice was beside him. He clung to her hand and watched her feverishly.

"Is everything all right?" asked Robert.

"Yes," said the girl.

"I haven't made a fool of myself?"

"Don't be a silly child. Go to sleep!"

He wakened next morning with a clear brain, the fever quite gone, his nerves soothed, his strength returned. The poison had been drawn from his cheek, and the swelling reduced. There sat Beatrice Larkin, looking just as fresh and pretty and untired as though she had not had an all-night vigil. Robert looked up at her with worship, and suddenly Miss Larkin looked away.

54

She went to the window and stared out.

"You're a lot better," said she. "If you're quiet all morning, you may be able to come downstairs this afternoon. Are you all right now?"

"It's as though I'd been on a long journey," said Robert. "With you, I mean. I hope—I hope I didn't say a great many foolish things?"

The merest tinge of pink appeared in the face of Beatrice Larkin. "Oh, of course you didn't," said she, and left him. But he was not reassured. The memory of spoken words remained in his mind, as though he had been saying: "Without you I shall die! Without you I shall die!"

He got up and dressed with some difficulty, and went down the stairs with oddly unsteady knees. However, he had the consolation that Beatrice Larkin had said that everything was all right, and that he was a hero.

He did not dare to examine that idea in detail; yet in the mid-morning, he managed to walk out toward the corral, to have a sight of Pinto.

On the way he met the roustabout, the cook, and a cowpuncher; every one of whom hastened to corroborate their mistress's flattering estimate. Robert went on toward the corral, and gradually he began to see that, no matter how the fight with Gill might appear in his own eyes, his exploits of the day before were important things in the eyes of the rest of the world. Tom Gill had been taken to the distant town under a heavy guard, and once that celebrated person was in jail, would not history record that one Robert Fernald, son of Dixie Fernald, had captured him single-handed?

Pinto put back his ears at sight of his master, but when saddling was not insisted upon at once, he worked his way to the fence casually, indifferently, until his head hung across the bars. "You scoundrel!" said Robert. "You ran away with me!"

Pinto nipped his master's ear and then tossed his head as though overcome with fear and guilt. But he made no effort to run away.

Robert laughed. His heart was very warm.

"We're sort of used to each other, old horse," said he.

Dan Parker was not one to sit down and rest after such a beginning had been made in crushing the rustlers. He took ten good and true men into the hills; and in five days they were driving a horde of cows which the bandits had pooled in the upper canyons of the mountains, to wait for a good market. There had been glimpses of the outlaws who scampered away as fast as they could. For it appeared their spirit had left them with the departure of Tom Gill.

So, by the time that Robert was fully recovered, the results of his fight were apparent on every hand. Beatrice Larkin announced with joy that the banks were now only too eager to supply her needs. And now she planned to resume operations on the scale and style which her father had employed so successfully.

"And in three years," said Miss Larkin, "why, we'll all be rolling in money."

She made a point of saying this in the presence of Robert Fernald, as though she wished every one to understand his share in any success that might come to her. She had a plan whereby young Fernald was to be established in the lower mountains with a little group of picked fighting men. Shifting his quarters from time to time, he was to study the mountains and learn the location of the open or box canyons, as the case might be. In case of a cattle raid, fire signals by night or smoke signals by day would tell the sentinels in what direction the drive was heading and Robert with his outpost guards could rush to block the exit. For such a service as this, Beatrice Larkin would pay most handsomely. Not only in cash, but in other ways. For instance, she had extensive timber lands in those tall mountains, and if they were worked on shares, with Robert representing her interests on the spot, he would be on a direct road to high fortune.

There were two things that he must do before he accepted any post, however. One was to complete his pilgrimage to his father's grave; the second was to visit Uncle Jimmy Dinsmore and bring him sharply to task for his treachery. Miss Larkin was opposed to either absence. For, as she pointed out, Gill was not the only formidable cattle rustler in the world, and all that kept others from establishing themselves was the fear of this new force in the Larkin valley.

Days slipped rapidly away while Robert strove to make his decision. There was nothing to mar the calm of his life now except that Pedrillo Oñate was expelled from the bunk house as a crook by the Larkin cowpunchers. They would have taken more violent measures if it were not that they held his master in awe. Robert called the man before him.

"Oñate," he said sternly, "have you cheated the men in the bunk house?"

Pedrillo raised his hand to the sky above them. His voice trembled with emotion.

"Ah, señor," said he, "when luck runs to a man, is it not true that others grow unhappy? They drove me out and would have murdered me and robbed my dead body if it were not that I belong to my little father, of whom they are very much afraid!"

Robert was sure that Pedrillo was a good man. And yet shadows of doubts persisted in crossing his mind.

In this unhappy quandary, he walked past the house into a lane of pine trees, where the fallen needles deadened the sound of his footfall. The unkind god of chance brought Robert now suddenly within sound of voices.

One was the voice of Fitzroy King; the other the clear tones of Beatrice Larkin.

"But the little fool looks at you like a calf," said Fitzroy King. "It's intolerable, Beatrice. Really it is! I've hesitated to speak. I don't want to presume, but after all, a man wants to shield the girl he's engaged to from any—"

"From what?" laughed Beatrice. "Good heavens, Fitz, he's only a child! I feel like a nurse or a grandmother when I'm with him. I just pity him; and I have to talk seriously with the poor dear and make him think he could be useful to me here."

"Pity is the nearest neighbor to love," said Mr. King with the surety of the very young.

"Love little Bobby Fernald? Love that baby!" said the girl scornfully.

Then they came around the corner and straight in view of Robert. He had wanted to slip aside, out of their way, but somehow his feet would not walk rapidly. So here they were before him!

Fitzroy King uttered a stifled cry and leaped back. But Robert was not thinking of him. He was too miserable to do more than note the horror-stricken face of Beatrice.

He slunk away among the trees and made for the house. An agony possessed him—lest he should not be able to leave the place before Miss Larkin returned. He met Pedrillo on the way to the house, and sent the Mexican to prepare Pinto and his newly acquired mule.

He rolled his pack together, and hurrying downstairs encountered Miss Atkinson.

"My dear Bobbie! You seem altogether fit," said she. "What's that roll of blankets?"

"I have to leave suddenly—" said Robert.

"Does Beatrice know?"

"Yes," said Robert faintly. "She knows."

"Well," said Aunt Harriet, "you'll be back soon! But you don't look so well just now, Bobbie. You must sit down a minute. I think that you've upset yourself by carrying that heavy blanket roll—"

Now that the veil had been snatched from his eyes, Robert realized that Miss Atkinson was talking to him as though he were a child—and that all the others always had talked to him as though he were the merest boy.

"Here's Beatrice rushing up the path," said Aunt Harriet. "You'd better wait to see what she—"

"No, no!" said Robert. "I must go at once. Only, I want to thank you for your kindness to me. I want you to thank Miss Larkin, too. And—"

"Bobbie! What in the world are you talking about?"

Robert fled without waiting for another word to where Pedrillo waited with his mule and Pinto.

Side by side they rode away from the Larkin ranch house, and Robert thanked the trees which screened his fleeing form. But there was no pursuit; and he was both sad and glad that he was left alone.

"Señor!" said Pedrillo suddenly. "You are sick!"

"Use your spurs on that mule and stop talking," said Robert harshly.

Never had he spoken in such a manner to any one. Pedrillo, blanched with fear, drove his strong mule to a run, and they rushed headlong down the trail.

Wild, fierce thoughts stormed through Robert's mind. He heard again the words: "Pity—baby—calf!"

To him! To the son of Dixie Fernald!

But when they reached the edge of the desert that evening and made camp, when the distant stars began to burn through the evening haze, his mind grew pacified. The ache in his heart was less and less. But he knew that it would never disappear entirely.

Night came. Robert could not eat. He lay on his back with his hands behind his head. Pedrillo, unconcerned, consumed a double supper and sang a little between courses as he let out his belt.

The image of Beatrice hung in the darkness above Robert, for the eye of the mind sees both body and soul. He could understand everything more clearly now. She was not to blame. She was above him, beyond him. Assuredly she had not meant to wound him. And his love for her grew more perfect because it was hopeless.

So by a touch of natural magic he recovered his faith in womankind; but there remained the terrible breach in the strong wall of his faith in men—there remained the cruel treachery of Uncle Jimmy Dinsmore.

Robert set his teeth and reached for the handle of his automatic. And fell asleep.

11

A certain recklessness had grown up in Robert's heart and his attitude toward his fellow men.

He said to Pedrillo as they jogged across the desert next day: "What is the name of the town where you were living, Pedrillo?"

"San Joaquin," said Pedrillo.

"Point us back for it then," commanded Robert.

"Señor, señor! They would tear us both to shreds!"

"Point us on to the back-trail for that town!" reiterated Robert.

Pedrillo, filled with thoughtful misery, obeyed.

In due time they sighted the wretched handful of hovels which rose like heaps of burned mud out of the sands.

"I wait for you here!" whined Oñate.

"You ride in," said Robert cruelly. "You ride in ahead of me. I shall come behind!"

Oñate began to whimper. "You can find trouble enough here!" said he. "You can find trouble enough without using me as bait while you fish for it! Do not drive me in!"

A silent gesture herded him forward, and Pedrillo went on like one condemned to death.

But Robert seemed merely to take a grim pleasure in his companion's pain. He relented not, and they rode through the main street until there was a loud shout, and Pedrillo, with a shriek of terror, fell backward from the saddle into the dust.

Then Robert saw on the sidewalk the ominous form of Charlie Bent, gun in hand, shouting: "Crawl over here, and lemme see what—" Charlie Bent left his sentence unfinished and leaped backward through the swinging doors of the saloon.

He had caught sight of Robert; and as he leaped he fired wildly into the air.

Robert missed Mr. Bent by an important fraction of an inch, but split the swinging door from top to bottom. Otherwise, there was no harm done, though Pedrillo was writhing in the street as though both shots had taken effect in his body.

Robert dismounted and entered the saloon, gun in hand.

To the rear there was a sound of many hastening feet, trampling through the exit, and voices raised in wild confusion. But in the barroom there was no one save a white-faced bartender, his hands above his head, who cried: "You ain't gonna murder a harmless man?"

Robert took stock of the situation with a mirthless smile. Then he called: "Pedrillo! Pedrillo! Come in here!"

Pedrillo rose from the dust and came in, shuddering with terror. He dreaded nothing in this world so much as he

61

dreaded his young master. And the sight of his obedience was a balm to the soul of Robert. He tapped with the muzzle of his gun on the bar.

"Pedrillo will have a drink," said he.

With a shaking hand, the bartender poured the potion.

"Drink!" said Robert.

"Yes, señor!" gasped Pedrillo. And he drank.

"What is your name?" asked Robert of the bartender.

"Dick Jones, sir."

"Dick Jones, Charlie Bent drew a gun on my friend Oñate just now. If it were not that I have very important business on hand, I should follow Bent and get an explanation from him. But I am busy and riding fast. I want to tell you that Oñate has come back to live in this town, and live in peace. If word comes to me that anything has happened to him, I'm coming back to learn the details. Will you let San Joaquin know that?"

"Yes, sir," said the bartender. "In your own words, sir."

Robert shook hands with Pedrillo, who was beginning to understand what was happening around him.

"Good-bye," said Robert. "Be honest, Pedrillo. But if you have trouble, send for me."

Pedrillo looked at the quaking bartender; he listened to the beat of horses' hoofs departing.

"Ah, señor," said he, "I think I can live the rest of my life in this town and never have trouble with any man!"

Ten minutes later, Robert rode through the desert on the farther side of San Joaquin; the past was behind him, and in the future he saw only the face of Uncle Jimmy Dinsmore.

In due time, he reached the hilltop and looked down on the recumbent form of his "uncle."

"Get up!" said Robert, in the harsh voice which he had used since that day when he overheard the conversation of Beatrice and Fitzroy King. "Get up and talk!"

Mr. Dinsmore got up, his mouth gaping open in amazement.

"Why, Bobbie—" he began.

"You've robbed me," said Robert brutally, "of sixty thousand dollars. Where's the money?"

Mr. Dinsmore staggered back. One hand grasped at the tree trunk for support; the other went toward his belt.

"And keep your hands free from mischief, sir," said Robert, watching narrowly. "I don't want to be tempted— any more than I am at the present moment!"

Mr. Dinsmore gasped: "Thief! I'm called a thief! And by a lad I've labored, planned, hoped for—good heavens, it's enough to kill a man!"

"What's become of the money?" said Robert firmly.

"You wouldn't believe me," said Mr. Dinsmore. "I'm a thief, so I'm a liar, too, I suppose!"

"If you have anything to say," said Robert, "I'll listen."

"Robert," said Mr. Dinsmore, "you ask me for sixty thousand dollars!"

"Yes."

"I'll tell you where it is in one word."

Even without a single word Dinsmore was able to say it. He made a sweeping gesture with both hands, indicating eloquently enough that the money had flown.

"It's gone?" said Robert, his eyes narrowing.

"It's gone!"

"Well?"

"You never knew Dixie Fernald," said Dinsmore. "But I knew him! You never held his head in your arms while he lay dying—but I did! 'Do for the kid everything that I'd do, old partner!' said Dixie Fernald to me."

"Well, what would Dixie have done?"

"I'll tell you!

"He would've kept on the way that he started out doing. He would've stacked up money on top of money, and he would've made himself so terrible rich that there wouldn't have been ten men in the country to hold a candle to him. I knew that's what Dixie would've done, so I says to myself:

'Doggone me if I don't try to do the same thing for this here kid. Little thanks I'll get if I just keep the money in the bank at four per cent!' So I started out to make that sixty thousand grow. Well, kid, I had no luck. I worked and planned and never invested a penny without thinkin' it over first and getting the best sort of information. But the fact was that I just had no luck. And nobody can get along without luck, and you ought to know it! Supposing that you had had a little bad luck instead of good? Suppose that Tom had had a little good luck instead of bad? Suppose that the bullet that knocked him down had been a quarter of an inch wide, and the slug that nicked your cheek had been centered a mite more? Suppose that had happened? Then you wouldn't be here to ask your Uncle Jimmy what he done with the money that he hoped to grow into a million or two for you! No, you wouldn't be here calling me a liar and sneak, and a thief and—"

Dinsmore ended with a groan. Robert looked at the ground.

Suppose that he were wrong?

"Look here! You blew in ten thousand gambling before you left the town where my father died. You blew it in inside of twenty-four hours!" said Robert.

"I?" cried Uncle Jimmy indignantly. "Who dared to say so?"

"Tom Gill."

"Tom Gill?" said Dinsmore, a little staggered. "Well, he was right. I blew in ten thousand. But how did he dare to say that it was your dad's money?" He gathered more force and warmth. "It was my own coin!" cried Dinsmore.

Robert gasped.

"Is that true?" said he.

"True? I'd swear—"

Robert raised his hand. "Don't swear," said he, "I want to believe you. I don't want you to perjure yourself just for the sake of convincing me. I could do nothing even if you *had* spent money that belonged to me. But as it is, I want to believe, Uncle Jimmy, that you didn't do it. I want to believe that you were true to Dixie Fernald!"

"Ah, lad, and I was! And even bad as I done, I got you through school, I guess?"

"You did," said Robert heartily.

He swung to the ground and limped forward.

"Shake hands, Uncle Jimmy, and forget that I've been talking like this if you can!"

Dinsmore took the proffered hand, but he took it weakly. He was pale and shaking.

"I can never forget, kid," said he. "Bein' doubted by you, that's a lot worse than I ever thought would happen to me. A lot worse!"

"I was wrong," said Robert sadly. "I never should have believed such an accusation against you, Uncle Jimmy. But I've had some hard knocks—I've learned to doubt nearly everything. I'm not made of the stuff that you and some of the old-timers were made of. I'm not so trusting! There's bad in me, Uncle Jimmy," said he. "And there's more weakness and badness than people guess, even!"

"Weakness?" echoed Uncle Jimmy.

"Aye, and I mean just that! Shall we go down and cook a snack?"

They had supper in the house as in the past. All during the meal Uncle Jimmy was as brisk and as cheerful as ever he had been. And after the meal, he launched into a glorious story about Wild Bill and Buffalo Bill and himself.

"Didn't Wild Bill die when you were just a child?" asked Robert, suddenly remembering another bit of Gill's evidence.

"Him? Wild Bill? Oh, you mean Hickock?" said Uncle Jimmy, his voice wavering a little and then recovering. "Of course he did! The Wild Bill I'm talkin' about was Wild Bill—Smith. Of course! Doggone me, kid, you wouldn't think that I'd mix up the two of 'em, would you?"

Robert breathed a great sigh of relief. He could listen to the story after that. But though it was as perilous as ever there was something lacking. Robert had tasted reality, and fiction would do no longer. And when he heard the soft snoring of Uncle Jimmy, Robert slipped from his bunk and sat beneath the stars.

He could breathe more freely, more happily, there; and suddenly he knew that he could not go back to spend the night in the shack. He left a note in the cabin; then he saddled Pinto, tied his blanket roll behind the saddle, and started across the hills. He had not the least notion where he was going. He wanted to turn his back on all the things that he had been. He had failed, he felt, most signally. The world praised him for defeating Tom Gill, but he himself knew the fear that had been in his heart. So he rode on this outward trail, asking only that he might encounter some adventure on such a scale that he could prove his courage to himself.

12

Catalina, sitting half seen among the trees, beckoned Robert Fernald with a scattered gleam of lamps among the shadows. And down he determined to go, and had loosened the reins to let Pinto pick his way through the stones and the shrubbery when he heard the clatter of hoofs behind him, and from among the great stones cantered a lean-ribbed mule bearing a ragged, round-faced, one-armed Mexican, who waved his single hand and shouted with joy.

"Señor Fernald! Señor Fernald! God is good!" cried he. "Little father, I have found you at last!"

There had passed many a lonely day and solitary journey since Robert parted with this man, and his eyes lighted as he took the hand of the Mexican.

"You never should have left San Joaquin," said Robert. "Tell me, Charlie Bent has frightened you out again?"

Pedrillo, had he two hands, would have rubbed them together. He rubbed his stomach instead—a fat stomach, which bulged against the pommel of his saddle—and chuckled softly.

"Ah, no, little father," said Pedrillo. "I lived in San Joaquin as safe as a branch on a tree or a rock on a mountain. Every one in that town is my friend, and Charlie Bent bought me a drink every day to show that he had no hard feeling against me or against you, señor. But money is not like seed; it does not grow; and presently all that I had was gone. Then one day as I sat in the sun thinking, that tall, strong man from Larkin Valley stopped his horse near me. When the dust had blown away from my eyes, I saw who it was."

"It was Dan Parker," said Robert, with a faint smile of pleasure.

"It was he, señor. 'Where is your boss?' said he. 'I am a free man,' said I. 'Free from work,' said he. 'But where's Fernald?' 'He has vanished,' said I. ' "Vanished" is the right word,' said he. 'I've been riding for three weeks trying to find his trail, but he's gone. Pedrillo, if you can get this letter to him and bring him back to Larkin Valley, you'll never be without a place to hang your hat for the rest of your life.' I listened. It was not the fine promise that stirred me. What did I wish in the world so much as to be again with you? The blind wish for sight, do they not? So have I wished for you, little father. I took the letter. I rode like mad on this poor mule. I hunted like a hawk on the wing and I have not rested, slept, or eaten since I started a

67

month ago. But here I am. All the hardships are as nothing now."

Robert looked at the fat paunch of the Mexican, but something more important than Pedrillo Oñate was in his mind. He took the envelope which Oñate extended to him, ripped it open with feverish haste, and read the strong, masculine handwriting:

DEAR ROBERT FERNALD: You know that when we think aloud we say all sorts of things, and a lot that we don't mean really. I was terribly humiliated that day when I found that you had overheard. But I was more sad than ashamed, and I still am. I want you to come back so that I can show you I'm not such a shallow, ungrateful person as you think now. There are selfish reasons, too, for wanting you here once more. The same canyons that made a good camping ground for Tom Gill promise to attract other rustlers who may not be so famous, but who can steal just as many cows. You see that I am shamelessly frank. I need you so that I can apologize; and I need you for the sake of your name and fame.

I want to say other things. But I know that protesting with pen and ink doesn't do much good at this distance. Only I feel like a child at school asking the teacher to give him another chance. Please give me that second chance, Robert Fernald.

Aunt Harriet wants me to send you her warmest good wishes; and whether you come back to us or go on your own way without forgiving me, may the best good luck ride with you.

BEATRICE LARKIN.

When Fernald had finished reading this letter for the third time, he was able to fold it, replace it in the envelope, and slip it into a coat pocket; though he still kept his hand upon it, as though to make sure that it should not slip away from him.

"Miss Larkin is married by this time?" said Robert, looking at the ground.

"Married?" said Oñate. "No, señor. And Señor King has left the valley and gone back to his home in the East."

Robert looked up. All the West was on fire with the

68

sunset gold and crimson. It seemed to him that never had there been a more appropriate burst of color.

"We take the back trail at once, then," said he. "Or, tell me, Pedrillo! You know every pass and hill and trail in these ranges. Is there no way of cutting through the mountains and reaching Larkin Valley in a straight line from this place?"

Pedrillo groaned at the mere thought.

"There is a way," said he, "but even the eagles hardly dare to take it, and they—"

"We'll ride that way," decreed Robert.

"Ah, little father," cried the Mexican, "consider that I have not eaten a true meal in this month of hard labor—and there is Catalina only a step away, waiting for us with tortillas, and beans cooked with peppers and tomatoes, and tender roast kid, and—"

"Silence!" said Robert, sweeping the summits with a restless glance. "Where does our trail start?"

"Besides," said Oñate, suddenly changing the nature of his appeal, "if we take the short cut, your horse will need grain in his belly to climb the rocks; and as for my poor mule, my poor Pancho—you see that even now his knees sag. His stomach cleaves to his back! One night in Catalina, and then we shall ride together—"

The coming dark, the high mountains, and the starved look of the Mexican's mule decided Robert. He turned his face toward the village in the valley.

"Very well," said Robert. "We'll ride down, Pedrillo. And in the morning we'll be on the up-trail before the dawn begins!"

So they wound down the steep mountainside and into the damp, dark forest. When they reached the Catalina River the last of the sunset light was gone. Over a staggering, creaking bridge, they reached the farther bank and the village which straggled there.

It was supper time in Catalina, so the street was empty;

even the dogs were indoors, waiting for scraps, and the only sounds which Robert and his companion heard were the noises of clattering kitchen pans as they passed; or the stamping and snorting of horses beginning to work on their filled mangers.

It was a crisp night, not altogether so cold as in the upper peaks, but the river damp hung in the air and a chill began to settle downward from the monster trees. They were not the fortune of Catalina, those trees. Far off in the mountains were mines of copper and lead, so the trees were not felled except to build houses. And what houses they were! The mountain winter could beat them with its fierce winds or heap its snows around the walls but never trouble the sheltered happiness which lived behind those thick walls of logs.

The heart of Robert expanded with joy. His happiness was welling up within him; he had cast despair behind.

"Tell me, Pedrillo," said he, "that you never have seen a town as happy as this Catalina. The honesty and the goodness of these people shine out of their very houses."

13

The hotel was seldom so crowded.

"You can chuck here, of course," said the proprietor, "and you can throw your blankets in the yard if you want to. Or you can go next door and tell Austin Bede that you want a couple of beds. He's always glad to pick up a few pennies. We're full here, though. Carl Lovat's back, and everybody's come in to have a look at him, of course!"

In the dining room—for they decided to eat before they

looked for quarters—Robert had sight of Mr. Lovat entering; a nervous, sharp-spoken man of forty-five with a clean-shaven face that looked a good deal younger.

"Who is he?" asked Robert, lingering a moment with Pedrillo.

Pedrillo did not know, and he was too filled with expectancy concerning the coming meal to spend any of his energy guessing. So Robert merely gave him a last warning as they parted, the Mexican to the kitchen for his supper, and Robert to pass on into the dining room.

"No one that I know is here," said Robert. "And I don't wish to let my name get about. Remember that. If any one speaks to me by my right name I'll know that you've let the cat out of the bag. Do you hear, Pedrillo?"

Pedrillo nodded and sighed. How much of the wild talk that went through the mountains concerning Robert Fernald originated from these fancies of Pedrillo, who could tell? But it made Robert vastly uneasy. He still had not proved himself *to* himself, and the terrible question haunted him: was he, indeed, a brave man?

That question clung in his thoughts as he entered the dining room at last, and settled himself to thin slices of fried steak, fried potatoes, fried beans, fried sausage, and fried pudding. It was not a tasty meal, and it was seasoned with drafts of the terrible mountain coffee, black as night and terrible as the furies. Down the leathery throats of the frontiersmen who sat around him these viands went in a flood; but Robert looked at them in dismay and hardly could touch his meal.

There was plenty to occupy him besides the food, however. He had to regard the faces of the men who crowded that table. The laughter was like rolling thunder, and the eyes of these unshaven wild creatures flashed terribly.

The heart of Robert sank more and more. These men did not regard him more than to give him a smile as to a helpless child who had wandered into their midst.

He wanted to leap to his feet and shout: "Don't despise me! I'm Robert Fernald! You've heard about me. I'm the man who captured the great Tom Gill. I'm the man who pacified San Joaquin!" But if he did, some one might look at him with a sardonic smile and say: "We know all about you, kid! That was just a lucky shot that dropped Tom Gill. Don't try to talk like a man when you're still no more than a boy!"

At the head of this long table sat Carlisle Lovat. When he spoke, all listened. By degrees, Robert began to learn the story of this man. Lovat had been born in the little town of Catalina. He had spent his youth here; then gone away to school; and though he had returned after his school days, he went back again to the East and there built up a great fortune. It was as a millionaire that he returned to the village.

Robert, staring at him, wondered what power lay in money that all these men should revere him so greatly.

In the middle of the meal, a squat, wide-shouldered man, swaggering into the room, went up to the head of the table! No sooner did he approach than the sheriff, his star blazing on his coat, started up from his chair and called out: "Berners, I'm watching you! If you're here to make trouble for Mr. Lovat, I'll let you know that—"

"He sent for me," said Berners, "or I wouldn't have gone out of my way to talk to him. You sent for me, Lovat. Well, what do you want?"

Robert looked closely, not at Berners, but at Lovat. As for the wide-shouldered man in the rough clothes, he had spotted him instantly for what he was—a gun fighter of a more or less old and unfashionable type. For whereas the more modern dandies of the six-shooter carried their weapons securely lodged under the coats, this man wore his strapped against his leg, so that though they might make uncomfortable walking they were constantly at hand for a quick draw. He wore them very low down on the thigh; the butts struck the palms of his hands, and his fingers could twitch out the Colts instantly. And Robert knew that he was another of those wandering spirits who "lived by the gun."

He turned, instead, toward the millionaire, much interested by the manner in which Lovat might take the approach of the ruffian. The rich man showed no fear. He merely leaned forward a little in his chair and looked keenly at Berners with a faint smile of interest.

"You're the same sort, Laurence," said he. "I see that you've grown up to your promise!"

"Is that a slam?" aksed Laurence Berners, resting his hand on the back of a chair, and never keeping his glance fixed on any member of the group at the table, but letting it wander restlessly here and there. "Are you knockin' me? I tell you, Lovat, that what you got to say ain't any more to me now than it was when we went to grammar school together. I could lick you then, and it looks like I could lick you now even easier. The rest of 'em in here may kowtow to you and kiss your boots, but I ain't that kind, old-timer. And if you've just called me in to look me over, you've had your look and I've had mine, and I dunno but what you've had a chance to see as pretty a picture as you've showed me!"

"Blowed-in-the-glass!" murmured someone near Robert.

And that described the vicious nature of Mr. Laurence Berners. His ways had been thoroughly vicious for so long that they were a part of him.

Mr. Lovat, however, did not respond at once to the insulting speech. Instead, he toyed for a time with a large silver cruet which graced his end of the table. It was a most elaborate cruet, such as Robert had never seen before. An enameled tortoise supported a tree, and the massive branches of the silver tree contained the apertures through which the flasks fitted. This treasure had been admired by Mr. Lovat during the meal, and he still touched it as he

73

regarded Laurence Berners with a keen glance. There was neither fear nor anger in his look. Instead, there was a sort of fascination and amusement—even a dash of respect.

"I sent for you because I wanted to see you; having seen you, I'd be glad to talk with you," said Carlisle Lovat.

"Talk up," invited the gracious Berners.

"Not here. In my room at Bede's."

"Why should I wait on you there? I ain't a servant of yours, and I don't owe you a penny. As a matter of fact, I'm as good a man as you are, Lovat."

"Or better, perhaps," Lovat smiled.

"Or better, perhaps," repeated Berners aggressively.

"Very well," said Mr. Lovat; "but nevertheless I think that you'll be waiting in my room when I get back to the house. That's all, Berners!"

So, dismissing Mr. Berners as if he were a hired clerk, Lovat turned back to his meal. It was very well done. It left Berners balanced first on one foot and then on the other, until finally he vowed, with a curse, that he never would stand about in the room of any man waiting for an interview. With that he slouched from the dining room. But Robert had no doubt that the gunman would indeed be found in the room of Lovat when the latter was ready for him.

And a question rose in Robert's mind. What did the rich man want of Laurence Berners? What honest use could any one make of such a person as Berners?

14

When Robert left the dining room—before the rest had finished, and while one of Mr. Lovat's tales was in progress—he went straight to the adjoining house of Austin Bede. The lower portion of Mr. Bede's place was given over to his silver shop, and the window, even at this hour, was uncurtained and illumined by an oil lamp, the burner turned low. Behind the glass, Robert saw a glimmering array; some articles, such as candlesticks and many little figures of animals and men.

It pleased Robert to see these things, just as the heart of a child is gladdened by the sight of toys. He was about to turn away when he heard voices at the door of the shop, and the subject of conversation was so extremely intimate that he hesitated to advance boldly upon the speakers.

He heard a man saying: "All right, I'll run along. But kiss me good night, Chollie."

And a girl answered: "Say, what a lot you take for granted, young man!"

"Aw, quit it, Chollie," said the man "You're gonna marry me, and you know it!"

"I know nothing of the kind."

"Aw, but you do."

"Why should I? Dad's dead against it."

"He thinks I'm a loafer," replied the undaunted Tim, "but you know that I'm not."

"You've hung around town and not turned a lick for six weeks," said the girl. "Ain't that the dodge of a loafer?"

"I quit work," explained Tim, "to take the job of makin'

love to you. And doggone me if it ain't been enough to keep the hands of any two men filled!"

"Keep quiet, Tim. Half the town can hear you boomin'!"

"Let 'em hear," answered he. "Don't try to be mysterious with me, Chollie. I love you; you know it; the whole town knows it; why shouldn't I tell 'em about it? Let 'em hear!"

"Tim Cavaselle!"

"Look here, Chollie; if you get crusty like this, I'm gonna kiss you good-bye instead of good night!"

"I'll slap your face."

"That's fair enough."

There was the sharp clap of a hand against bare skin, and then the noise of a well-planted kiss.

"Tim!" gasped Chollie. "I hate you like a snake."

"Aw, you liked it, Chollie. Don't lie to me. Good night, sweetheart."

"I—I hope you—"

She could think of no wish bad enough to fit his scandalous case.

And then: "If that skinny runt, Lovat, is making eyes at you I'll run him out of town the same's I did Dick Fraser."

"Don't be a fool," said the girl. "I wouldn't marry a bank like him. He's nice to me. That's all. Just because he used to court my mother."

"Just because he's set his cold eye on you. Well, I'm gonna give him a warning. I heard him talkin' to your old man about setting him up in business in New York. Does Lovat ever do something for nothing? No, he don't. What does he want back? Why, you. That's plain!"

"Tim, you're an absolute fool!"

"You take it pretty hard," said the outright Cavaselle. "I guess I've touched a tender spot. But so long, Chollie. Wednesday I get your final answer."

"All right, Tim."

"And I know what it'll be, honey."

"You know nothin'!"

Tim Cavaselle laughed loudly, and started to walk down

the street; in so doing he passed Robert, paused, and then clapped a heavy hand on his shoulder.

Robert found himself looking up to a youth of the most heroic proportions.

"You been hearing something, kid?" asked Tim Cavaselle.

Robert was too taken aback to reply for a moment; then he stammered that he had been about to enter the house, but had not wished to interrupt such a conversation.

"The heck you was!" said the blunt cowpuncher. "All that you done, then, was to hang around and eavesdrop, eh? But I'll tell you, kid, I don't give a hang if the whole world was to hang around and hear what I've got to say. But—if I catch you doin' this again, I'll take off all your skin and hang it up to dry and make socks out of it."

He turned away from Robert, and went whistling down the street, so little malice did he carry in his outspoken heart. As for Robert, he trembled with excitement and anger at being addressed in such a manner, but he had been unable to think of a retort for the big man, before the other was fifty long strides away.

And, with fallen head, he went to the door of the shop which the girl was just closing.

She was made on lines ample enough for an Amazon. A big, good-natured, smiling, cheerful girl she was.

"Hello, bud," said she. "What you want? Buying something for your best girl, maybe?"

Robert, a little embarrassed, managed to declare that he was not, and that he wanted a room, and for that night only.

"We'll fix you up," said the girl. "Maybe you could do with half a room, eh? Or d'you aim to take full-sized man's quarters?"

Robert drew himself up to the full of his five feet and eight inches.

"Madam," said he, "I need a room, or a bed, or whatever you can give me!"

"Hello! Hello!" said the girl. "Aw, don't get huffy. Step in and sit down, will you? I'll run up and see who's in for the night."

She went off and left Robert in a little back waiting room, at one side of which the owner of the place and the father of Chollie sat at a deal table on which a number of silver articles were displayed. Opposite him was a well-dressed gentleman smoking expensive cigarettes.

He held raised in his hand a little silver model of a broncho, lump-headed, hump-backed, ewe-necked, but with legs which, even in the silver, looked all their iron strength and endurance.

"Or this," said the stranger. "This, now, would be a nice trinket to give to my youngster. What sort of a price do you put on this, Mr. Bede?"

Austin Bede was a huge man, mightily bearded and with eyes half lost behind a downfall of gray eyebrows. But his shoulders slumped forward and his back was curved out in the fashion of one who has hung over his work too many hours. Yet there was manliness in his face, and in his big, workman's hands there was manifest great power still.

"I'll tell you," said Austin Bede. "There's hardly more'n enough silver in that to make it worth more than—fifty dollars, say?"

"Fifty? Hello! That's rather steep!"

"But as a matter of fact, I don't really want to sell that. I'd rather keep it, Mr. Norden."

The other pushed back his chair with an exclamation.

"Very well," said he. "I see that it's no use trying to do business with you, sir! You want to keep all of your best work. And—"

He paused, as though recollecting himself with an effort.

"I'll have to find other Western trinkets for my family!" said he. "Tell me—how much of this stuff do you sell in a year?"

"Not enough," admitted the silversmith sadly, "to pay for the metal that I have to use. Not enough!"

"Then why won't you sell now?"

"Look!" said Bede, taking the silver horse. "I know how other people make these things. Where I served my apprenticeship, any man could turn out some sort of a horse in a week. But the fact is, sir, I spent three months on that horse!"

"Very odd talk," replied Norden, "for a silversmith in this part of the country. By the way, how did you happen to settle down here?"

"I found my wife here," replied Mr. Bede. "She liked this part of the world. So I settled here."

"And let your business go to pot?"

"She liked this part of the world," said the silversmith.

"But after she died? If you went to a big city—"

"It would be a bit queer to move away," replied Bede. "You can take the work with you, but you can't take the country that I got the ideas from."

And he indicated the silver figures: the horse, a mountain goat walking on a dizzy ledge wherein a three-inch cliff of silver was made to give the effect of a dizzy precipice, and a band of antelope behind which, with some artful foreshortening, one was made to guess at the limitless flat of the desert.

Mr. Norden rose.

"My good friend," said he sharply, "it appears that you have formed the habit of working for your own pleasure and not for sale. And in the meantime, you let your daughter support you by taking in lodgers. Is that the idea?"

The silversmith flushed. His large head sank a little, and he sighed as he touched the delicate form of an eagle perched on a crag of black rock.

Mr. Norden, grim with indignation, stalked angrily from the room and at that moment the girl came back.

"Well, Dad?" she asked eagerly.

Her father shook his head.

"What? Nothing?" asked Chollie, vastly disappointed.

"He wouldn't buy," said the father, "nothing except these."

He indicated some of his chosen treasures which stood on the table.

"But you could have sold one of them at least," suggested the girl.

Mr. Bede allowed his head to fall still farther.

"No difference!" exclaimed the girl cheerfully, throwing her arm around the massive shoulders of her father. "We'll make out some way. They can't do any more than turn us out of the house!"

The big hand of Austin Bede went up and closed over the arm of his girl.

"I'll find money some way," said he. "I'll find it some way—before morning!"

He said it calmly, but it was a desperate calmness. So that before Robert's eye there was conjured up a terrible picture of attempted robbery, of drawn guns, of battle!

"Ah, I forgot about you!" said the girl, turning suddenly to Robert. "I've found a corner for you. It doesn't amount to much, but there's a bed in the place. Will you take a look?"

Robert was shown to a little chamber which was hardly larger than a closet. It had one small window high up on the wall, and aside from a cot which filled half of the floor space it held no furniture.

However, it was a place for rest, and Robert accepted it.

"How much?" he asked.

"Aw, nothing at all!" said the girl. "We ain't low enough to charge a man a lodging for a kennel like this one! You take it and welcome, partner!"

"But," began Robert, "I—"

She was out of the room before his clumsy tongue could frame the words he wished to speak, and she left him alone in the semi-darkness.

Robert sat on the edge of his bed and buried his face in

his hands. He wanted to find some solution of the problem of the silversmith, and he hoped that if he concentrated some suggestion might come to him.

15

There was no great opportunity for Robert to continue his thinking, for it appeared presently that the room adjoining was that same back chamber in which Austin Bede was now sitting with his daughter, and every word they spoke passed easily through the thin partition.

"All that the devil could wish is true," said poor Bede. "I've failed right and left, Charlotte. I've piled up debts, lived almost on charity. I'm a worthless good-for-nothing!"

"I'd like to hear another man dare to call you that!" cried Chollie. "But we'll find a way out. I tell you, we'll get some money out of Carlisle Lovat. He's full of it. He's dripping with money, dad."

"Be quiet!" exclaimed the father. "D'you know Lovat? I do! You never could get something for nothing from him! Get five cents from him, and he'd make you pay for it with your heart's blood! That's his way!"

"You let me handle him!" said the girl.

"Charlotte, I command you not to ask him for money!"

"Well, we'll see about that!"

A very grim tone had the girl as she made her answer. At that moment, without any preparatory knock, the front door of the shop was thrown open.

"Who's that walkin' in so big and bold?" Robert heard the girl murmur.

He heard the voice of Carlisle Lovat: "I've brought the sheriff along to hear what I say."

"Evening, Sheriff Minter," said Bede. "Take a chair."

"I met your friend, the cowpuncher, on the street," said Lovat. "I mean Cavaselle. And he told me that he intended to run me out of town if he found me in this house again. Did you authorize him to say that?"

"Of course not," replied Bede.

"I thought that you didn't, and I told him so. He was angry and threatened me. I told him that I was not a fighting man, but that if it came to a pinch, fight I would and could; and if he killed me, he would hang for it if money could hire good lawyers. I've repeated all this, Charlotte, not because I'm afraid, but because I mean what I say. And I suggest that you pass along the word to Cavaselle yourself, my dear girl."

All this was spoken almost dryly—certainly not in the manner of one greatly afraid of what might happen to him in the future.

"There'll be no trouble," said Bede hastily. "Tim's a good boy, I think!"

"Good, is he?" interrupted Sheriff Minter. "I got to tell you folks that he ain't so good as you think. He's killed his man. He's killed his second man. And he's killed his third. Down in Arizona they don't act so kind and cheerful with him as we do up here. He's threatened people before. And he's killed before, too! Oh, fair enough fighting—but a killer is a killer. You might let your friend know what I know about him, Charlotte!"

"Send your own messengers!" snapped Chollie. "If you want to backbite Tim, do it to his face!"

"Spitfire, Chollie. That's what you are," chuckled the sheriff. "Now, Mr. Lovat, what's next?"

"I'm going up to my room," said Lovat. "And there I expect to find Laurence Berners waiting for me. Sheriff, I'd like to have you wait for me down here, if you don't mind. I haven't much to say to him; but what I have to say may make him pull a gun. I'll just ask you to leave this door open. If you don't see me coming back in ten minutes by your watch, make a break for that room, because the business I have to talk over with Berners shouldn't take more than half that length of time!"

It pleased Robert to hear Lovat talk. For whatever the business was which took him to Berners, Robert gathered the impression that danger of death never would turn back Mr. Carlisle Lovat.

"You know the sort of a man you'll be talking to," warned the sheriff.

"I know him like a book," declared Lovat.

And with his crisp, brisk step he left the room.

"He's got plenty of nerve," murmured the sheriff in admiration. "Berners hates him, too."

"Why?" asked Bede.

"Dunno. Berners hates near everybody."

They talked of other things, quietly, calmly. And yet Robert knew that they were thinking of the same thing that made him, from time to time, look at his watch.

But their nerve was better than his. Two men and a girl sat in a room listening for a gunshot, and never once did they betray the slightest anxiety. For his part he counted the minutes trailing slowly away. Eight minutes, nine minutes—

"I think I'll just be stepping upstairs," drawled the sheriff.

"I'll go along," said Bede with equal calm.

"You stay where you are!" snapped the official with decision. "I'll do this job by myself—"

Here a door slammed in the distance. They heard loud voices. Heavy steps came down the stairs.

"I've told you what I'll do," said Lovat. "You take it or you leave it. Understand?"

"I'll see you hanged. You will be hanged!" howled Berners. "You skinflint, you rat!"

"Swear yourself out of breath and back again," replied

the other contemptuously. "But in the meantime, don't forget that I have made a proposal to you."

"A low-down, cheap, five-cent—"

"Berners, think it over. You'll be back in the morning to say yes."

Berners, stamping in his fury, rushed through the room and out of the house.

The sheriff wished to know now if Mr. Lovat were perfectly at ease in the town, or if he desired protection of any sort.

Lovat's answer was delivered in a drawling voice: "I'm in danger every minute of my stay here, sheriff. But I don't want any more protection."

The sheriff departed.

"That was a funny way to talk," said Charlotte, large in accent as in person. "How's your life in danger in this town, Mr. Lovat?"

"Wait a minute till I get back. I want to hear the answer," exclaimed the silversmith. "I'm going for my tobacco."

As his heavy footfall died away, Lovat said to the girl: "I think you can guess where the danger comes from, Charlotte!"

"Not me!"

"Perhaps, I'm growing old," said Lovat, half serious, half ironical. "But it seems to me that I'm in a good deal of peril. In the first place, there's Berners. He's a dangerous creature if ever there was one. In the second place, there's your father—"

"My father!"

"Look at this ring of mine, my dear. Look at the red stone in it. That's a ruby, Charlotte. And that stone is enough to keep the wearer in a good deal of danger no matter where he be!"

There was a little silence. Charlotte was not committing herself.

"Your father is broke. Worse than broke. That ruby alone would pay his debts and put him on Easy Street for a while.

Now, Charlotte, suppose that he should get it into his head to put a bullet through mine in the middle of the night and just slip this ring off my finger—"

"Carlisle Lovat," said the girl, "I don't mind a joke, even if it's a mighty bad one, but don't talk like that about my father. Why, he'd never hurt a chicken!"

"Wouldn't he?" chuckled Lovat. "Very well. We'll hope not. But in the third place, I stand in danger from young Tim Cavaselle, who is not such a fool and braggart as I took him to be. He really is capable of murder, it appears!"

"You fill the whole town with murderers," said Chollie, yawning audibly.

"Of course I do, my dear," said the rich man. "And in the fourth place, I'm in danger from you."

"Hullo! Go on and tell me!"

"That's what interests me," said Lovat. "I was only joking when I first talked to your father about marrying you, but now that I begin to take it seriously—"

"Don't be the only serious one about it," said Charlotte coldly. "Who wants you to be serious?"

"The truth is, my dear," said Mr. Lovat, "that you are amazingly handsome, and I can't help thinking about you."

"You're making love, I see," said Charlotte, with another yawn.

Robert felt that he was not listening to a love scene at all, properly so-called. It was rather a sheer revelation of character.

"Yep," replied the girl. "It's pretty funny. You'll laugh about this later on, I know. But you won't laugh alone, Mr. Funnyman!"

"By heaven!" said Lovat with warmth. "I like you better and better."

"Swearing, too," said the girl. "That proves that you come from the West!"

"You young minx," said Lovat, with his inevitable dry, rattling chuckle.

"D'you want me to listen to you?" asked Charlotte.

85

"By all means."

"Then tell me what in the world should make you want to look twice at a girl like me?"

"Youth and good looks, my dear—" began Lovat, only to have the girl cut in loudly.

"That string's worn out, Mr. Lovat. Quit it, will you? I know! With your flock of money you could pick out something flying high and handsome. Don't tell me I got the looks!"

"Haven't you?" asked Lovat, not pressing his point at once.

"I'm not so bad," answered Chollie. "I'm better on a horse than I am on foot, and the first flash of me is better than having me opposite to you across the table every morning and night. But you tack another fifteen years on me and I won't be much to boast about. And you know it. So what's the line and what's the game, Mr. Lovat? I'm curious."

"Suppose that I call you Chollie?" said he.

"I don't care what I'm called. Go ahead."

"It pleases me a good deal to call you Chollie. Well, Chollie, the reason I'm more and more interested in you is that there's no bunk about you. You hit from the shoulder and—"

"And that's your own style, I suppose?"

"No, not entirely. Sometimes I'm blunt. But not often altogether honest. I'd be a poor man today if that were the case. But, Chollie, I don't give a hang for society and small talk! Not a hang! You and I would have a couple of friends. A good many acquaintances. I'd be good to you. I'd be specially good to your father."

"I suppose you'll say you're fond of him?"

"Not a bit. But I'm fond of you, and keeping him afloat would make you stick to me."

"I like your line of talk," said the girl. "It's queer, but it's interesting. Go on."

"After a while, you'd grow interested in running my house, bossing my servants, and amusing me."

"And what about you?"

"I don't think I'd get tired of you. I'm old enough to know what I want. And I always get it; and I always keep it."

"Women ain't money, you know," suggested the girl.

"No, they're pretty much the reverse," chuckled he. "But if the worst came to the worst—why, marriage is not eternal, in these days of Nevada, eh? A divorce never would break your heart. But I'd make you so comfortable that you wouldn't think about it a great deal."

"Interesting, all right. But it don't buy me, Mr. Lovat."

"Why not? Tim?"

"Yes."

"You love him, eh?"

"He's such a great idiot. Sure I love him."

"Do you think that that ends me?"

"I think it comes pretty close to ending you."

"Not a whit. One rarely gets what one wants at the first try. I'll simply find a way of raising my bid."

"Still talking money, eh?"

"Not altogether money. Just think this over. So will I. Tomorrow we'll talk again."

"Whenever you say!"

"Hey, Chollie!" called the voice of her father in the distance.

"He can't find his tobacco," said the girl. "I'll have to get it for him. Coming, dad!"

Mr. Lovat departed; the girl ran to her father; and Robert lay down on his bed without so much as taking off his clothes.

He did not intend to fall asleep. He simply wanted to close his eyes and review matters in greater detail to see what he could make of them, and this singular combination of Berners, Lovat, Bede, Cavaselle, and Chollie.

But it had been a long day; he had ridden far. Before he knew it, he was soundly asleep. And he dreamed an old dream, of riding through the streets of a town where people on either side pointed at him and smiled behind their hands. A most unpleasant dream which had made him groan in his sleep on many a night before this. He was awakened by the sudden crash of a gun, and a loud scream that stabbed the night, died, and left the world listening!

16

He leaped to his feet and flung open the door of his room. Not a sound in the house! Fear shut off his breathing. A door slammed, and Robert started so violently that it forced a groan through his set teeth. He could not tell from what direction the sound had come. From the outside, he rather suspected!

He did not wait to get out the front door of the house, but climbed out of the narrow window, set high in the wall of his little room, and dropped ten feet to the ground outside.

There, as he crouched, he saw the broad-shouldered, squat figure of a man climb down the side of the house, apparently handing himself down by a drainage pipe that ran to the roof.

Laurence Berners!

There were not two men in the whole world who had that apelike silhouette. Robert jumped to his feet and ran in the direction in which the shadow of the man disappeared among the shrubbery. He had barely entered the brush when a huge form towered before him, crashed into him, and knocked him spinning. The gun spun from Robert's hand as he fell; and he heard a deep voice growl a curse as the big man plunged on his way without a halt.

Half-stunned as Robert was, he recognized the voice of Tim Cavaselle, the cowpuncher, and lover of Chollie.

By the time he had recovered himself and found his gun, he decided that it would be foolish to try to follow Berners at once. He turned back to the house where now a tumult of voices sounded and heavy running to and fro. He entered by the rear and spied a light through a crack in the kitchen door. To that crack he put his eye and looked in through a narrow vista. What he saw was enough to curdle his blood.

For there was Charlotte Bede working with a frantic haste first to reload an emptied chamber of a Colt revolver, and second to clean out the barrel, so that all signs that the weapon recently had been used might disappear.

Could a girl have fired the shot that caused that scream of terror?

Aye, such a girl as Chollie! Now, with her teeth set and her eyes gleaming with determination, she looked the perfect type of warrior.

Robert, sick at heart, and utterly bewildered by this time, hurried along the hall. When he came to the stairs, he found a new subject of wonder.

For down those stairs came Sheriff Lew Minter, and before him he drove a tall man whose hands were shackled, a tall and dignified man who was none other than the silversmith, Austin Bede!

"What's happened?" asked Robert of some one who stood by, ferret-eyed with a malevolent interest.

He got no answer.

"Hal!" called the sheriff loudly.

"Aye, aye, Lew!" came the answer from above.

"Don't touch the body—don't let nobody touch it till I come back!"

"Right, Lew!"

The sheriff went on with his prisoner, saying to him: "Just you watch yourself, Bede. I don't aim to handle you mean unless you make me! Just you watch yourself, will you?"

The silversmith said nothing. There was a quiet dignity about him. He stood straighter and he walked with a light, strong step. He looked fifteen years younger than when Robert had seen him last. He looked capable, indeed, of shooting to kill!

But now a stream of the curious began to hurry up the stairs and Robert joined the stream. At an open door on the floor above the current pooled itself in a closely packed crowd which stared in at Hal, the deputy, seated on a disheveled bed with a naked Colt in his hand, watching the door.

In the center of the room, face down, a gun loosely gripped in his right hand, lay the body of Lovat, the millionaire. And a little red pool had welled from his heart.

Robert drew back and leaned against the wall, feeling very sick, but able to listen to the comments of the bystanders. From their words he gathered the story of what had happened, at least the sheriff's viewpoint.

Lew Minter, disturbed by various things, had decided to be near the house of Bede all of that night, with the result that the instant the shot was fired, and before the scream had ceased ringing through the night, the sheriff leaped silently up the rear stairs of the house and came to the door of Mr. Lovat's room. He reached it just in time to meet Austin Bede coming out, and he had arrested the old fellow on the spot on the charge of murder. For one glance inside the room had showed Lovat lying dead.

Motives? The motives were plain! Lovat's wallet and

rings, representing a considerable fortune in themselves, had been stolen.

Mystery? Aye, there was mystery, too. For the treasure was not found on the person of the silver worker. The only solution was that he must have thrown his loot through the window of the room into the grass of the yard. So the yard was searched, but not a sign of any booty was found.

Now all these things were done in a very short time, and Robert hurried to the jail, where the sheriff had barely secured his prisoner and appointed a guard to watch over him. Most placid did Austin Bede appear in the cell. To those who crowded against the bars with questions, he returned brief, gentle answers.

Robert managed to confront the sheriff. "I have to offer a little testimony, sheriff," said he.

"About this shooting?"

"Yes, sir."

"Jeff!"

"Aye, Lew."

"Take down what this gent has got to say. Come in here!"

They went into the sheriff's office. The crowd buzzed and hummed outside. And Robert told, clearly and with a painful exactness, just what he had seen: how a man who had the outline of the famous Laurence Berners had come down the drainage pipe; and how, in pursuing him, he, Robert, had crashed into the fugitive form of Tim Cavaselle and been knocked to the ground in the collision.

The sheriff grinned a little, but then looked serious.

"And how did they get out there so fast, if they done the killing, either of them?" he asked.

"Could you run up the stairs," countered Robert, "as easily as a man could slide down the drainage pipe from Lovat's room?"

The sheriff was silent, biting his upper lip.

"I'll round up Cavaselle and Berners, both of 'em," said he. And he hurried out to issue his orders.

But though many men hastened to obey these commands, neither Berners nor Cavaselle were apprehended. They had disappeared from Catalina with singular speed, and the search of the sheriff bagged no trace of them.

There was other evidence which Robert could have given, but he could not find it in his heart to tell how he had seen the girl, Chollie, in the kitchen cleaning and reloading a gun. However, he had done enough to throw considerable doubt on the guilt of the silversmith.

And by noon of the next day, every one agreed that Bede could not be punished for a crime which might conceivably have been the fault of two other men, both of whom were missing. The important thing was to find the pair of them.

And now Robert saw his duty before him as clear as the face of a shining star!

Business was at hand. Robert had guessed at the proper thing for him to do. The sheriff himself made the suggestion with a proper earnestness.

"Fernald, you're interested in this case. You think that old man Bede didn't do the job. Well, why not help to prove it? We can't prove that Cavaselle or Laurie Berners is guilty if we haven't 'em handy to charge with the crime. They're gathering a jury to try Bede. They'll hang him, too; you can be sure of that! Now, suppose that you was to start out on the trail of 'em, and try to bring in one of those fellows. You can have your pick of the best men in the town. I swear you in as a deputy—you understand?"

"I understand," said Robert faintly. And he began to grow pale, and paler.

The sheriff stared. He knew now that here was a celebrated young man, reputed fearless. And yet the young man trembled and turned white! What was to be made of such a thing?

The sheriff waited. He dared not make up his mind about such a matter on the spur of the moment.

"How many men would you suggest that I take as a posse?" asked Robert Fernald.

"A dozen. Take a dozen of the best. You might need 'em."

"But," said Robert, "if I took a dozen, the other men that we're chasing—they wouldn't have much of a chance, would they?"

"A chance? I don't know what you mean."

"Well, I mean, that they would never have the slightest chance against such a number of men, sheriff. And then, you see, it wouldn't be good sport to chase them with such a crowd. It wouldn't be fair. Isn't that clear?"

The sheriff looked at his companion with eyes that opened wide. He was seeing something more than the boyish, smooth, pink-and-white face of Robert Fernald.

"Would the hunting of those two men be sport to you, my lad?" he asked.

Robert considered gravely.

"Not sport—but a duty, you know," said he, hunting for words to match the emotion which was within him. "But if you were being hunted, sheriff, you would want to have your chance against one man instead of a dozen, of course. And there's no honor, you see, in running down a single man with numbers!"

The sheriff at last understood; and he smiled a little, his eyes shining.

"It's reputation that you want, Fernald," said he. "I can understand that. Though I should think that what you did with Tom Gill would last you for a while. But if you prefer to tackle this job by yourself—why, it's a fact that one man makes less noise and dust than twelve!"

Such was their understanding before Robert Fernald was sworn in as a deputy and given a little certificate which entitled him to act in the name of the sheriff.

Then Robert went to the stable behind the hotel, and found Pinto dancing in his eagerness to be out. Not that the little horse was a lover of work, but he hated the indoors with a consuming hatred. Then Robert sent for Pedrillo and his mule.

The Mexican came in fine fettle, for he had enjoyed himself greatly in Catalina since the announcement of his master's identity.

"If you were in love with a pretty girl in this town," said Robert, "and you got into a fight here and killed a man, what would you do?"

Without a moment's hesitation the Mexican answered: "I should ride as fast as I could to the house of Juan Patron, up yonder in the mountains, and ask him to let me hide out near his shack."

"Is Juan Patron an old friend?"

"Yes."

"What good would it do you to be so near?"

"Because it would be as hard for them to hunt me near as to hunt me far off. Besides, they would be very likely to override me. And also, I should have a chance to slip back into Catalina from time to time to see the girl I loved—"

Robert had heard enough. He made Pedrillo wait while he went to make inquiries which soon gave him an embarrassing richness of information.

Cavaselle had friends near Catalina. Yes, he had scores of them. It appeared that every man in the mountains either was a friend or an enemy of Cavaselle. There were no neutrals.

"But his best friends?" asked Robert, at his wits' end.

"Old man Dodge, yonder by the Sugarloaf; and Chris

Hansen on the opposite side of the valley in the narrows between those two summits."

Old man Dodge, it appeared, had instructed the fatherless Cavaselle in the arts of hunting and trapping, and Robert felt that the fugitive might have taken shelter with such a time-tried ally as that—if, indeed, the cowpuncher were not far, far across the mountains before this. So he and Pedrillo rode out of Catalina, and passing down the main street, Robert was hailed by a strong voice: "Hello, Bob Fernald!"

It was Chollie Bede, walking with her long, masculine stride and carrying a basket.

Robert reined his horse closer to her and raised his hat.

"Is your father terribly worried?" he asked.

"You'd never guess it," said the girl. "He's sitting in the jail smoking his pipe; and they've let him have some stuff to work at, so he's as happy as can be! Or at least, he lets on that he is!"

"Give him my kindest wishes," said Robert. "And tell him that I know he is innocent. I—I even hope that I may help to prove it!"

"The deuce you do!" said the girl. "How would you manage that, then?"

"By finding the man who did the shooting."

Chollie whistled.

"More power to you," said she. "I'm taking Dad his lunch, and I'll give him the good news. You're a kind fellow, Bob Fernald!"

"Ah, no," said Robert. "Only, I think that I can tell the good people from the bad, you know!"

She shook hands with him, giving him a powerful grip, and Robert passed on up the street. All this was not exactly as he had imagined it. He had expected terror on the part of the prisoner, tears on the part of the girl, but this was no world of tales or books in which our Robert found himself.

Up toward the Sugarloaf they made their way, he and

Pedrillo, with Oñate extremely uneasy. They climbed for a little over two hours, and then came to the edge of a pine wood and looked into a rough little swale of ground partly set out in a vegetable garden, with a patch or two of grain growing. In the midst, with tall brush all around obscuring it, was the shack of old Dodge. And there was Dodge himself sawing up a supply of firewood!

Robert reined swiftly back into the woods, and Pedrillo followed softly on his mule. The eyes of the Mexican were big with curiosity and fear when they reached a little clearing in the trees, and Robert halted.

"Señor, we have become hunters?" he asked.

"We have become hunters," he admitted. "Man hunters, Pedrillo. Can you help me in a pinch?"

"I can help myself, señor," said Pedrillo, turning green-yellow with unhappy thoughts. "But you cannot ask a man with one arm to help others! I have only this old gun!"

As he spoke, he pulled from its holster beneath his right leg a short-barreled shotgun of large caliber.

He looked the picture of woe, and Robert smiled at him. In a way, he was glad to have such a coward along with him. It set his own uncertain nerves against an excellent background.

"Now, Pedrillo," said he, "I am going to stay here with the horses. I want you to steal up around that shack and watch it like a hawk, until dark if you have to, or after dark. See if there is any other person in the little house, and if there is, come and tell me about his looks."

"You will not make me fight, little father?"

"Not a stroke. Go and watch cleverly and come back to me safely. I don't want to lose you, Pedrillo! What should I do without you?"

Pedrillo was as pleased as a child by this compliment. He went off with his eyes shining. So perfectly did he enter into his part that one step from the edge of the clearing, he vanished from sight. In the distance Robert could hear the whine of the long saw as old Dodge drew it back and forth through the tough, sappy wood. Near by the leaves shook and rattled now and then; and noises of flying insects whirred loudly into his ears and faded. Robert was beginning to sink out of the strenuous, muscular world of action where naught but great things or brilliant thoughts are possible, into the passive world where the senses awaken so that we are placed in harmony with life itself, whether the life of a fungus or the life of a mountain.

In this mood he heard the crunch of a footfall, louder to Robert than the crashing of heavy guns. He sat up with a start, and the parting of the shrubbery opposite to him showed him the huge shoulders and bulky figure of Tim Cavaselle!

18

Robert remembered the old story of the wishing gate, which is at hand when we know it not. Yonder was clever Pedrillo, using his Indian craft to locate a possible second person in the house of Dodge. And here at hand was the wanted man, stumbling fairly upon Robert!

Tim Cavaselle saw the stranger in the clearing as he strode forward, wrenching himself through the brush like one who has such an excess of strength that he need not worry about cunning. He saw, and he reached for his gun, but Robert had jerked out his ugly-faced automatic in the least part of a second, and leveled it at the other, while

Tim's hand was still gripping the butt of his gun, half-unsheathed.

Cavaselle hesitated. He knew nothing of the identity of this young man. But he could not despise that leveled weapon.

"Don't make your draw, Cavaselle," warned Robert. "You'll be hurt if you do!"

Cavaselle growled. He was growing red with anger.

"What's into you, runt?" he asked impolitely. "What's into you? What you want with me?"

"Unbuckle your gun belt," requested Robert.

"Kid, you're makin' a fool of yourself."

"Unbuckle your gun belt!" said Robert. "I tell you, Cavaselle, you murdered a man in Catalina and then ran away and let an innocent man be jailed. I'd shoot you down with no more compunction than I'd shoot a woodchuck!"

Mr. Cavaselle hesitated, a black scowl upon his brow. Then he obediently unbuckled the belt—obediently but slowly. The belt and its revolver and heavy hunting knife fell to the ground.

"Walk over to the center of the clearing," said Robert, getting to his knees without removing his attention from his captive.

Cavaselle obeyed, more slowly than ever.

"It ain't really possible," he declared. "It ain't really possible that I've been snagged by a baby-faced boy like you! Now, what you want?"

The sound of the saw in the distance ceased.

"Talk quietly," said Robert. "I don't want to alarm Mr. Dodge. But I want you to go down to Catalina with me. I want to put you in the jail there and take poor Austin Bede out!"

"Bah!" snarled the big man. He strode nearer, menacing.

Now that Robert was on his feet, and his lack of inches was revealed, Tim Cavaselle's scorn increased every moment.

It made the blood of Robert leap. He felt terror at the

nearness of the huge cowpuncher; and yet that terror was not unpleasant. It kept a singing of delight along his taut nerves. This was the spice that life needed.

"Don't come too close, Cavaselle," he warned.

"Suppose I tell you that I'm not coming down with you?" asked Tim Cavaselle. And he clenched his fists.

"You're not a madman, I hope."

"Well, I'm big enough to take a slug through the body and get in at you," said Cavaselle. "And once I laid my hands on you—why, I'd tear you in two!"

"I doubt it," said Robert, the striking muscles quivering along both his arms.

"Are you nutty?"

"I think I might even handle you without a gun," said Robert, his breath taken by his own temerity.

At the mere idea of such an encounter his brain fired with dread, with horror, with terrible joy. And his lips began to twitch; his eyes began to glitter.

Here was a handicap of a full sixty pounds over and above his own scant hundred and fifty. But against that handicap, he might stack his long training in wrestling and boxing.

"You might even handle me without a gun?" sneered Tim. "Kid, I would tie one hand behind me and still be ashamed of hittin' you! Why, I'd—"

Robert slipped from his coat, and, weighted by the gun it contained, it fell heavily to the ground. He stepped forth into the very shadow of his foe, looking slenderer than ever in his shirt sleeves.

Cavaselle laughed. He scanned Robert from head to foot and laughed again. For he was a little too excited to be accurate in his observations. He saw the pink-and-white cheeks of Robert, but he failed to see the economy and neatness with which Nature had framed Robert, and all that Nature had given Robert he had improved wonderfully.

Yet Mr. Cavaselle did not see this.

"The kid has grit, after all," said he, as though to an audience. "But I wouldn't know how to begin with you, son. It'd be like hitting a girl!"

"This will take away some of your scruples," suggested Robert, and stepping lightly in, he struck Tim across the cheek with his open fingers.

"*Aghr-r-r!*" snarled Tim Cavaselle.

And he smote at Robert, a good, whole-hearted, sledge hammer stroke.

It missed! By the proverbial yard, it missed. Robert smiled a little, with white, twitching lips.

"I'll kill you!" said Tim, seeing that smile.

He rushed in and smote again. Furiously, with either arm he struck, with arms that had been steeled by labor all his life. But he could not find his mark. It floated before him. He no longer missed by yards. By fractions of inches he failed, and it seemed as though the very wind of his punches was driving before him the frail object of this attack, as a gossamer shred floats from beneath a striking hand.

So Cavaselle smote and grunted and raged and fumed. He drove Robert back across the clearing until the little man's heel struck a root and down he went. Have you ever seen a cat trip and fall? So Robert tripped and fell—and whirled to his feet again faster than a bouncing ball.

But honest Tim had not striven to take advantage of this opening to throw his weight upon his elusive foeman. Instead, he gave back, scowling and cursing, and saw that Robert was fairly planted upon his feet before he charged again.

Robert, however, had been stung to the quick by fear and surprise. He no longer retreated. Under the sweeping arms he ducked, stepped in to meet the heavy rush, and with his right fist he drove to the jaw of Tim Cavaselle. He did not sweep or hack or carve like Tim in his fighting. But he hit from his toes, so to speak timing his weight, his lifting power, his energy of nerve and body and hand and leg so that all exploded at the correct instant. And the explosion hit the correct spot: about an inch from the point of the jaw, where there is a full lodgment for the knuckles, and where a properly applied shock is transmitted, with all the effective leverage of the long bone of the lower jaw, to the base of the skull.

Tim Cavaselle turned halfway round. His rush was stopped. His power was gone.

He began to tremble and sway, like a great tree which has been cut to the inner core by the ax. His head rolled on his shoulders. His knees bent, sagged, gave way. And he dropped upon them, fumbling at the ground with one hand. His spirit was not beaten or overawed. He cursed the blackness that swam across his brain, and shook his head to clear his wits. But Tim was totally upset, and Robert went to his coat and put it on. His knuckles were sore and were beginning to swell, but otherwise he felt no ill effects from the encounter. Yet he felt exactly as though he had been riding a storm wind.

19

By the time Robert had settled himself in his coat, Tim Cavaselle was on his feet, shaking his head like a great bull. But he showed no resentment.

"I understand, kid," said he. "You're a pug, though I'm hanged if you look the part. All right. You've got me. Now what?"

"We go down to Catalina," said Robert.

Tim Cavaselle made a wry face.

"Me with my hands tied, maybe," said he, "and you drivin' me in like a cow! No!"

Robert was amazed.

"You won't go?"

"No!"

"But look here," said Robert, "you have to, you know. I—have the advantage over you, it appears!"

"You've got a gun in your hands," said Tim Cavaselle. "Use it, then."

"Do you propose," asked Robert, his eyes very wide, "that I should shoot you down in cold blood?"

"Kid," said the big man, "we all got to die once. Today may as well be my time. But—I won't go down with you! If you come at me, I'll tackle you again, and though I couldn't beat you in a fair fist fight, I'll sure massacre you at rough-and-tumble!"

Robert regarded Tim Cavaselle with a frown of bewilderment.

"I don't know what I'm to do," said Robert at last.

"Think it out for yourself," answered the big fellow. "I'll take my medicine and never yelp, you can bet!"

Light dawned on Robert.

"It's the girl," he said suddenly. "You don't want to be shamed before her, of course."

"Would you?" asked Mr. Cavaselle.

"No," admitted Robert, "I certainly wouldn't. As a matter of fact, I respect your attitude, Mr. Cavaselle. But how am I to get you to Catalina? And tell me man to man—did you kill Lovat?"

Cavaselle looked at our hero partly in cunning and partly in amusement.

"Want me to confess right now and pave the short road to a hanging party?" he suggested.

Robert blushed.

"Well," said he, "all that I can do is to take a long chance, it appears. I have to shoot you down here in cold blood—and I don't want to do that. Or else I have to take your promise that you'll go down to Catalina and give yourself up. Or—"

"Would you trust me to go down and give myself up?" asked the cowpuncher curiously.

"I think I would," said Robert. "Or—we might take an even start and shoot the thing out."

Tim Cavaselle cast a quick glance toward the spot where his gun lay.

"Do you mean that?"

"It might be a good idea," said Robert, "if you shoot quite well!"

"What?"

"You see," explained Robert seriously, "I am rather an expert with guns. I've spent a great deal of time trying to become one, at least!"

Tim Cavaselle burst out: "Well, I'll be hanged, kid, if you ain't the queerest lot that I ever come up with! Suppose you lemme see how much of an expert you are? There's a fool blue jay sitting on top of that sapling yonder. You might take a drive at him."

"Certainly," said Robert without hesitation.

Instantly the automatic flashed into his hand and exploded.

The tip of the sapling was shorn away under the feet of the astonished bird, which dropped a yard downward and wheeled on the wing—wheeled just in time to receive a second bullet that tore through its body.

A crimson wreck, it dropped heavily to the ground.

"I was a little too hasty with the first shot," said Robert, flushing. "But the distance was so short and the bird so big—you see, I was a little overconfident!"

Tim Cavaselle measured the "short" distance with an accurate eye.

"Kid," said he gravely, "you and me are not gonna shoot this thing out with guns. Because you *are* an expert. So am I. But you got me beat. Well, you got nearly everybody beat!"

"Oh, no," said Robert.

"Oh, yes!" said Cavaselle. "I know! What might your name be?"

"My name is Robert Fernald."

"*What!*" Cavaselle broke into loud laughter. "All right," said he, "if you're Fernald, that settles it. Fighting I don't mind. But I sure hate suicide. Fernald, if you'll trust me to go down to Catalina, I'll start right pronto and go down. And what's more, I'll tell who it was that sent me."

"But you don't need to," said Robert earnestly. "It might embarrass you, and besides, it would count more in your favor if it were thought that you had given yourself up willingly!"

"You talk more friendly than hostile," remarked Cavaselle.

"With all my heart," said Robert, "I hope that you come through this affair with no trouble. I hope that you're innocent. I—I really think you are!"

"If it wasn't me, then it was old man Bede, of course."

"Bede? Oh, no. There was the third man. There was Laurence Berners. I should have started after him in the first place."

"Is Berners mixed up in this?"

"Yes."

Mr. Cavaselle whistled, and then exclaimed: "And you're going after him?"

"I suppose that I shall have to," said Robert seriously, "if you're not the guilty man."

"I'd give ten years of my life," declared Mr. Cavaselle, "and I'd give 'em gladly, if I could have a chance to see you and Laurie Berners mix it! There'd be a grand scrap, and nothin' much to choose between you."

104

"I hear that he's a really terrible man," said Robert, his eyes growing larger, as they had a way of doing.

"Him? Well, they say a good deal about him, but nobody ever has said enough!"

"No?"

"I should say not! Oh, I know all about Berners. I've seen him in action. And I was in Tracy right after he killed the three Sherry brothers. I walked into the room and seen the bodies laid out. The three of 'em had come to get him. He didn't even jump for cover. He fought it out with 'em, and he salted 'em all away!"

"He killed all three!" breathed Robert.

"Sure, he did. They put four bullets through him. But he's harder to kill than a grizzly. You got to find either the brain or the heart to stop him. His brain is so small that you could easy put it into a walnut; and as for a heart, why, the whole world knows that he ain't got one. You and him will have a fine go when you hook up together. I'd sure like to be on hand!"

"I suppose that I must take up his trail," said Robert, paler than ever. "But it frightens me a good deal just to think of it!"

"Frightens you?"

"Oh, yes. My blood is ice, just to think of it."

"Well, have you got a grudge against Berners?"

"No."

"Then why do you go at all?"

"The sheriff asked me to help," said Robert weakly.

"Humph," said Mr. Cavaselle. "But look here, old-timer, did it ever occur to you that maybe you was doing this job because you like danger?"

"*Like* danger?"

"Ain't that possible?"

"I never heard of such a thing!"

"The things that we like the most ain't always the sweetest," said Cavaselle. "Whisky ain't very smooth, but we drink it. Whoever liked the first taste of beer? And the same way with danger. Me and most, we stay away from it if we can. But there's some that get sleepy in ordinary times. They got to have something to wake them up. Why, old-timer, you're that kind! 'Danger,' you say, and you turn pale! But the more you think about it, the more you got to follow the hard trails! Ain't that correct?"

"I don't think so!" said Robert, much distressed.

"Well, but I'm right," declared Mr. Cavaselle. "And you'll keep on following the hard trails until you get a bullet in you one of these days. You'll get famous, but you'll die young!"

It was a very new idea to Robert. He considered it, and suddenly he could see that it was truth! No man in the world could fear danger more than he; and no man in the world could be more drawn by its fatal attraction.

So thought Robert, brooding upon the destiny which was drawing him forward. And he was more frightened than ever before. Except that hitherto events and creatures had filled him with terror, but now he was terrified of himself and of the powers which were working in him.

He looked up to Tim Cavaselle and sighed.

"Perhaps you're right," said Robert. "I shall never forget what you've said. In fact, I think I shall have to leave this country of guns and gunmen!"

"After you've finished this job, however," suggested Tim.

"Yes, of course."

Cavaselle smiled and said no more.

"Shall I start for Catalina?" he asked.

"If you will."

Cavaselle crossed the clearing, picked up his gun belt, deliberately strapped it on, and then left the clearing and proceeded toward the house of old Dodge.

20

Three days later, Robert and Pedrillo Oñate were on the far side of Catalina cutting for sign on a grand scale, as it were, and still without a trace of Berners to guide them, when a message came out to them from the sheriff of Catalina.

There had been strange occurrences at the trial, in the meantime. For one thing, Bede could give no good account of what had brought him to Lovat's room so late in the night. He claimed that it was a bit of local information concerning trails that Lovat had asked of him that he had suddenly remembered. But when the district attorney grilled him in cross-examination, Austin Bede had floundered lamentably and made an exceedingly bad impression upon the jury.

Now matters were rapidly focusing. It had been proved by the district attorney that Bede was staggering under a heavy burden of debt and that the jewels of Lovat would in themselves have been enough to cancel all he owed, to say nothing of the contents of Lovat's wallet. And then, most crushingly, it was learned that three of the debts, totaling more than five thousand dollars, had been paid off by Bede's daughter a short time *after* his arrest. How had she come to have so much money?

When Miss Bede was put on the stand and questioned she simply said that her father always, to a certain extent, hoarded money, and that after his arrest he had ordered her to take what he had in savings and with it discharge his three largest debts. She had done what she was told to do. Otherwise, she could not make an answer.

She had been a good witness on the stand. But it was pointed out by the district attorney that it would have been utterly strange for Austin Bede to accumulate a hoard of five thousand dollars when he had been faced with utter ruin; and when several times he had postponed that ruin by making personal appeals to his creditors!

"Bede was a man who took in little cash, and who hated therefore to spend it," said the lawyer for the defense.

But the district attorney proved that, on the contrary, Austin Bede was an unworldly dreamer who cared not a whit for money, and who gave it away with ridiculous freedom. Furthermore, at the very time of the trial, did not the silversmith sit in his chair idly thumbing a bit of molding clay? Was this a man to hoard money?

The jury, by their expression, showed to which side they leaned.

Five thousand dollars suddenly had appeared in the possession of the defendant—appeared immediately after he was held on a charge of murder. Undoubtedly that jury felt convinced that the jewels and wallet of the murdered man had made up the sum.

So the coils were drawn closer, momentarily, around Bede. Day by day he sat in the courtroom and saw his chance for life disappearing, but never gave a sign of the slightest concern. And his tall daughter walked as bravely and unconcernedly through the streets of the town as ever before.

Such was the case when Cavaselle rode into the town and surrendered himself to the sheriff.

"What made you come down here and surrender, Cavaselle?"

"Fernald sent me."

It made a great sensation in the town: the power of Fernald to do the thing, the honor of Cavaselle in keeping his promise to Fernald.

But what had Cavaselle to do with the case? He was

questioned sharply. What had brought him up at such a late hour on the night of the murder?

He had been unable to sleep, and so he had gone for a walk under the stars.

The jury chuckled. In fact, Cavaselle did not look like a nervous man, or one who would lose sleep, or seek starlight for a consolation.

What really had made Cavaselle get up at that hour? He stuck to his first story. Why, then, had he fled after the murder of Lovat? He had not fled after it, said Cavaselle. He had decided before this that he would ride up to the cabin of his friend, Dodge, and get there by daylight. And that was what he had done. He had not known that he was suspected in connection with the trial until young Fernald told him so.

This tale disappeared in smoke before the district attorney's examination. For it was after the murder, of course, that Robert Fernald had blundered into Cavaselle outside the house. That being the case, what had led Cavaselle to lie in this fashion?

The jury was filled with interest, and the district attorney freely implied, by his questions, that he suspected Cavaselle of being in league with old Bede—Bede to do the murder, and Cavaselle to wait outside the window and receive the loot which the murderer would throw down to him.

Then Cavaselle had disposed of the stolen articles, and placed the money in the hands of Bede's daughter. Or even, suggested the district attorney, he might have placed it in the "hoarding place" and let the father tell his daughter about the money later on. In this manner, all suspicion of guilt would be removed from the shoulders of the girl.

The case was black against Bede. It grew blacker after the clumsy testimony of Cavaselle who, under cross-questioning, became sullen and silent and swore at the district attorney and vowed that he would not testify another word. He was put in jail for contempt of court, to stay there until he changed his mind about talking.

The district attorney had unearthed a further bit of valuable evidence as to the reasons which would impel the silversmith to take the life of his guest.

In the first place, it appeared that when Lovat was a young man in the town, there had been bad blood between him and Bede. Lovat had wooed the girl who married Bede. And now when he returned to Catalina, it was suggested by conversations which had been overheard, that Lovat had taken his lodgings in the house of Bede particularly in order that his display of wealth might humiliate his old rival.

Last of all, the proposals which Lovat had made for the hand of the girl were bared in the court. Rather than let his daughter sell herself for his sake, Bede would kill with his own hand and cut the Gordian knot of his difficulties.

It made a neat case. There was no doubt about the guilt. The only question was: What would the sentence be?

The jury found Austin Bede guilty as a matter of course, and recommended him to the mercy of the court—a recommendation which the court saw fit to overlook. For the judge pointed out that no matter what else could be said in favor of the accused and his long and blameless life, he had destroyed the life of a guest, and that was the greatest of great crimes.

He sentenced Austin Bede to be hanged by the neck until he was dead. And God have mercy on his soul!

This was the information which the sheriff sent in much detail to his valued deputy. And he added that if anything were to be made of the possible testimony of Laurence Berners, something would have to be done about it at once. What could young Fernald suggest?

110

21

It was a clear portrayal of the state of things in the town, and it threw Robert into a deep dismay. All that he had done in the sending in of Cavaselle seemed less than nothing. Berners he must get; and how should he go about it? There was no trace of the gunman. No one had heard of him.

Others did not regard this as important. For Berners would very frequently disappear in exactly this fashion, no doubt to appear again far off, do a work of mischief, and vanish once more.

But to Robert the thing seemed clear as the clearest sunshine. Berners had vanished because it was his hand that had struck down Lovat, the millionaire; his hand that had stolen the jewels and the wallet, and now like a black scoundrel, he allowed another man to be condemned for his sin! These were Robert's conclusions, and he wondered that others had not arrived at them!

If only he could get at Laurence Berners! And he said to Oñate: "Pedrillo, if you had two hands, and could shoot equally well with both, what would you be apt to do? If you could shoot straight and fast with two guns, I mean?"

Pedrillo had finished wiping the frying pan. Now he looked up to the lofty pines that rose above them.

"Ah, little father," said he, "if I had two hands once more and could handle a good gun in each of them, first of all I should go back to San Joaquin, to my own town, and there I should make certain men eat dirt before me!"

"So?" said Robert. "But San Joaquin is only a little town,

111

Pedrillo. If you were a great fighter, you would want to go to a bigger place and be a king over it."

Pedrillo considered this suggestion for a moment.

"Now and then," said he, "I would ride out to other towns. When I heard that there was a great man here or a great man there, hard fighters, terrible men, then I would ride out and find them. I would strike them down. I would ride over them. I would leave them for the wolves to eat, little father!"

"And always return to San Joaquin, Pedrillo?"

"Always to San Joaquin, señor. Because in that town, though it is small, I was born. And I know all the people. I know their values, as though they were so many coins in my purse. It is better to be a great man among those whom we know than it is to be a great man among strangers. So it seems to me, at the least!"

He lighted a cigarette, rolled Mexican fashion into the shape of a cornucopia. He leaned back against the stump and closed his eyes and turned the cigarette slowly between his lips.

"Very well," said Robert, "but now and then you would need money. How would you get it in that little town?"

"Those who have strong hands may take where they will," said Pedrillo. "Consider. Did you not ride into Larkin Valley and do one great thing, and would not the lady who owns the valley give half her lands if she could have you there to defend the other half? Would she not pay you much money?"

Robert bit his lip and was glad of the darkness which covered his blushes.

"Let us ride there, señor," suggested Pedrillo. "Let us go to Larkin Valley where we will be like kings in the land!"

But it was not Larkin Valley that Robert had in mind at this moment.

He regarded the dying fire; he looked at the solemn trees, gilded and made rosy by the light from the flames.

"Tell me, Pedrillo—do you know much of Laurence Berners?"

"Every wise man knows a wolf," said the Mexican. "You can tell it by its track. Yes, I know Señor Berners, because I have heard of him and I have seen him. Men cannot help talking about a wolf, particularly if it steals sheep from their cotes."

"What is his home town, or has he one?"

"Yes, señor. We all know what his home town is. He lives in the town of Last Buffalo. There was an Apache village there, and so it got that name in the old days. Why do you ask me, señor? May heaven forbid that you go hunting that man!"

"I have to go to Last Buffalo," said Robert. "Be ready for an early start. Is it far away?"

"A day's ride, señor. But what is to be gained there and what can be done there? Tell me, little father!"

It was plain that Pedrillo dreaded the native town of the gunman as others might dread a wasps' nest.

But Robert dwelt no more on his intentions.

"Suppose, Pedrillo," said he, "that you were away from San Joaquin and an enemy came to your home town, and that he rode up and down the streets and abused you and swore that he would kill you on sight. Suppose that case, Pedrillo; I mean, if you were the king of your town?"

"Ah!" snarled the Mexican. "It makes my blood rage to think of such a thing! As soon as word came to me that the scoundrel was doing this thing, I would come like the wind—"

"But suppose that you were far off, in hiding. Then what, Pedrillo? Suppose that it was necessary for you to hide because of some foolish thing that you had done—say the robbing of a stage?"

Pedrillo smirked. He was pleased by the suggestion that he might have the courage and the adroitness to rob a stage of his own prowess, unaided.

113

"Ah, señor, no matter what strong reasons I had for hiding, if I knew that a rascal was in my own home town defying me, scorning me, I would come furiously. I would kill horses in my haste. I would ride night and day, and when I came to San Joaquin, I would be sure to dash up to the saloon. I would ride my pony through the swinging doors. I would have a revolver in each hand. 'Where is the dog who asks for Pedrillo Oñate? Tell the fool that I am here, ready to kill him.' Such is the manner in which I would speak. And I would fill that fool and coward and braggart full of lead and have him buried like a dog in a trench!"

Robert, listening, shuddered a little. He slept little that night, but awakened again and again and stared at the clear, bright mountain stars high above, and the dimly glistening needles of the pines. But he knew the thing that he had to do, and he would not shrink from it. The bright face of danger drew him as the magnet draws iron.

Tim Cavaselle had been right!

The town of Last Buffalo had originally had every natural advantage to give it protection, and none to give it trade. It stood on a ridge in the midst of a narrow valley, with a streak of white water boiling at its feet on either side. Thus it had been in Indian days, when a tribe of copper-faced warriors made it their permanent headquarters. Then the white men came and took up their residence on the ridge.

After a while, they let their houses sprawl down toward the river side as soon as the law was strong enough in the land to make peril from Indians an unnecessary consideration. The twin rivers were bridged, the town grew richer. It grew greater. A fringe of houses sprang up on the farther side of each of the streams, close to the bridge heads. Along the ridge there was the usual village street—a single lane where the shops, the saloons, the hotel, and a few of the houses were posted.

Robert rode with his head raised, his face pale, his eyes melancholy, as befitted a man who was not, perhaps, more than a few moments from death. So they gained the single business street of the town, which wound uncertainly, following the irregularities of the summit ridge. There Robert stopped a youngster of fifteen who was riding past on a broncho, bare-backed.

"Is Laurence Berners in town?" he asked.

The boy brought his horse to a halt with a jerk on the reins. Through the dust cloud raised by the planted hoofs of the mustang as it slid to a stop, the stripling studied Robert.

"Are you a friend of his?" he asked.

"I've only seen him once," said Robert.

"Well," said the boy with a flashing grin, "you'd better not see him again."

And laughing loudly at his own impertinence, he galloped off down the street.

"He is right," said the Mexican eagerly. "You should not see Señor Berners. What could you gain from him except bullets and wounds, little father?"

They came to a blacksmith's shop, and Robert drew rein. The blacksmith, his forge room filled with milky smoke, was working up his fire. Robert, riding close to the door, leaned from his saddle and called: "I beg your pardon!"

That blacksmith left off his labors at the bellows handle. "What for?" he asked.

"I wish to ask you a question. Can you tell me if Laurence Berners is in this town?"

The blacksmith, in place of answering at once, stowed a fragment of tobacco in one cheek and then jerked his thumb over his shoulder.

"His house is right down the street. I dunno what's in it." He added gloomily, after a moment: "What's more, I don't want to know." With that, he turned his back upon Robert.

Robert murmured to Pedrillo as they continued on their way down the street: "I've never met such discourteous people, Pedrillo. What is wrong with them?"

"The questions which you ask them, señor. That is the trouble, of course."

Pedrillo chuckled.

"If you have a corn on your foot, señor, you do not like to have that foot stepped on."

Robert smiled a little wanly.

"Ah well," said he, "I must find out from some one!"

The house of the seemingly unpopular Berners stood not far off; a little white-painted cottage, exceedingly neat and trim, with a flower garden in front just beginning to give out spots of bloom here and there.

When Robert knocked at the front door, a tall woman with a face as hard as iron opened the door, and looked down on him from her commanding height. She stared at him coldly.

"This is the house of Mr. Laurence Berners, I believe?" said Robert, his hat politely in his hand.

The tall woman did not answer.

"I came to ask if Mr. Berners is at home?" said Robert.

"He ain't," said the giantess, and stepped back and slammed the door in Robert's face.

He was hurt and bewildered by this treatment, but he was exceedingly glad that Mr. Berners was not at home. He sighed with relief, and tapped at the door again. He tapped twice; the only response was the clanging voice of the woman from within: "G'wan and stop botherin' me!"

116

So Robert took a piece of paper from his pocket and wrote on it:

DEAR MR. BERNERS: When you come back to your home and receive this note, you'll know that I am waiting to take you to Catalina, where you are suspected of the murder of Mr. Lovat. I intend to stay in this town until you come to meet me, and when we meet I shall attempt to persuade you to go back to Catalina with me.

Yours most faithfully,
ROBERT FERNALD

When he had finished this note, he pushed it under the door and retreated rather hastily to his horse. For he had an unpleasant idea that the woman of the house—was she the mother of Mr. Berners?—might fling the door open and come rushing out at him.

Once safely in the saddle again, Robert jogged Pinto down the street, and poor Pedrillo in a panic at his side, stammered: "Señor, you are not going to have a thing to do with that Laurence Berners, are you?"

Robert made no reply. He only said, when they came to the hotel: "I want my name to be known in this town, Pedrillo. I have to make these people think that I'm a little more than a child, you see? And it will help if they know who I am. Not that I have done much. But you understand, Pedrillo, that people talk a little about the capture of Tom Gill."

"And the taking of that fellow Cavaselle," said Pedrillo. "But ah, little father, why should the people of this town come to fear you and to know you? Is it not better, if we must stay here, to live quietly, to trouble no one? For if Señor Berners should learn that you are here, might he not try to make himself greater by coming down and killing you as he has killed others?"

"Perhaps he may," said Robert. "Perhaps he may. I can't tell!"

He gave his horse to Pedrillo and went up the steps of

the hotel and presently was leaning over the register, writing his name.

"Robert Fernald? Robert Fernald?" said the fat proprietor, reading the name. "I've heard of it somehow, seems to me. But I guess I'm wrong," he added, looking narrowly at Robert again. "I guess that I sure must be wrong. Well, come along, pardner!"

And he showed Robert to a room, a back room, and a dark one, with one little window looking on the rear yard and its unsightly litter of trash and junk.

"What might you be doing in Last Buffalo?"

"I am waiting for Laurence Berners," said Robert.

"Like fun you are!" chuckled the proprietor. "Ain't you afraid that he might eat you when he comes, kid?"

"Perhaps he may," said Robert.

The proprietor paused at the door and looked back.

"Not aiming to buy his house, are you? Because doggone me if the old woman would move out of it!"

"Oh, no," said Robert. "I'm not going to buy his house. But I want to take Mr. Berners away with me."

"Take him away? Where?"

"To Catalina, to answer a murder charge."

"Hey, what the jumping—Look here, kid, d'you know who you're talkin' about?"

"I was given the work to do, you see," explained Robert humbly. "So I had to come."

"Kid, are you meaning to tell me that Lew Minter sent *you* up here all alone to get Berners?"

"Yes."

The proprietor gaped, and then he began to laugh rather blankly, like one who feels that a jest is in the air, though he cannot quite locate the point of it.

118

23

Pedrillo had become the master of ceremonies. And as such he did the talking for Robert, who refused to talk for himself. There was nothing that Pedrillo wanted less than a meeting between his master and Laurence Berners, but since he felt that the meeting was inevitable, he decided to make the most of it—which is always an excellent plan.

When it was known that *the* Robert Fernald was in town, and that he would not chatter freely about himself, all men resorted to Pedrillo. He had drinks free whenever he chose to take them; he became the most important figure in either of the two saloons; and an enchanted circle was held by his tales from morning to night.

Under his adroit handling, the manner in which Robert got Pinto and beat the former owner of that horse became a thrilling epic. And the story of how Robert chased and caught and captured the great Tom Gill was such a matter that Pedrillo could not get through it in a single day of steady talking.

To be sure, Pedrillo overstepped the mark a good deal in all directions, and at last the men of Last Buffalo were inclined to think that he was a windy chap with little truth in him. Then an odd event occurred which fortified all that Pedrillo had said and caused his word to be accepted like Gospel.

It happened that, on a day, he described how his master practiced with his guns and how he, Pedrillo, would throw up stones at which Robert tried snap shots.

And his master, according to Pedrillo, never missed.

"How big a stone?" asked a grim-faced cowpuncher who had handled guns all his life. "As big as this?" And he showed a shining chunk of quartz.

"Yes," said Pedrillo, "or even smaller."

"At thirty paces?" said the cowpuncher.

"Yes, señor. And that is truth by the—"

"Leave off your swearin'," said the cowpuncher. "You're a liar, and I'm gonna show the town how bad you lie!"

So said the cowpuncher and straightaway sought out Robert, dreaming on the veranda of the hotel. He covertly marked out thirty paces from the edge of the veranda into the street. And there he turned and sang out: "You gents!"

"Hello?" came from the idlers.

"I've got a little stone here, and twenty dollars to the gent that can nick it with a bullet when I throw it up. Who wants a try?"

Who would not spend a cheap bullet for the sake of a twenty-dollar note? All were willing, except Robert.

The end man of the line who sat in chairs along the veranda made the try first and missed; and the second and the third followed suit. But Robert slipped from his chair and made for the door of the hotel.

"Hold on, Fernald! Ain't you going to take your chance?"

"No," said Robert, "I—"

"You ain't afraid?" sneered the cowpuncher.

Robert hesitated a single instant, and then stepped to the edge of the veranda.

"Very well," said he. "Throw up the stone!"

And it was done, without waiting for him to make ready. Up spun the shining quartz and hung for an instant at the twinkling crest of its rise. The automatic leaped into the fingers of Robert. He had very little hope of striking the target. It was quite true that he made pistol play at just such marks as this, but it was even truer that he had rarely made a hit. However, it was better to try than to be shamed.

At the very instant that the stone hung at its height, he fired—not an aimed shot, but a snap from the height of his hip. As the gun boomed, the rock dissolved into a cloud of brilliant particles.

Robert went hastily into the hotel, saying that he did not want twenty dollars for a trick such as this. But the town of Last Buffalo gathered to talk over the deed and measure again the distance at which the shot had been fired.

Pedrillo, scared and silent, had watched the trial, well knowing what it meant. When he saw the victory, his joy knew no bounds. But he knew enough to control himself.

"Ah, señors," said he, "I would not see any man throw away his money in such a way. If you were to throw up such stones all day, my master would not miss three times. And those three times would only be because he was careless. You observed, my friends? He did not even aim. He fired from the hip."

"It must have been luck!" gasped the disgruntled cow-puncher, who had offered the money.

And a bystander remarked dryly: "The same sort of luck that dropped Tom Gill with a bullet down the side of his head!"

Pedrillo was invited back to the saloon. But now he had a more crowded and more attentive audience. Men listened with a grave interest. They had seen magic. They were willing to believe anything!

Pedrillo was not the man to miss such an opportunity. From that moment, his stories about his master became wilder and more brilliant; but the fictions were delivered with a graver and more matter-of-fact air. It would be hard to say how much of the great reputation of Robert Fernald can be traced back to these same tales, but certain it is that a large part of the wonderful stories which to this day are connected with his name must be traced to the glorious inventions of Pedrillo Oñate in the town of Last Buffalo.

When those stories were repeated, if any man sneered or

shrugged his shoulders, there was a crushing retort: "I'll tell you what I seen with my own eyes! I seen Fernald stand on the edge of the hotel veranda and a stone was throwed up a full thirty paces away—a stone no bigger'n this here. And Fernald with a snap shot from the hip, he blew that stone to bits. I seen that with my own eyes. And so did Ham Strickland, and Hugh Moore, and—"

One touch of reality redeems a world of nonsense. The fame of Robert was made in that instant.

People in the town had a continual question during the first few days. If Robert Fernald really wanted to find Berners and fight him, why did he not go hunting for that worthy?

The answer was both simple and spectacular. Pedrillo, of course, was the source of it. Robert Fernald knew that he could destroy poor Berners. But he didn't want to do it alone, in the desert. He preferred to work where men could see him. His private hope was that Berners would not be foolish and make a fight. Fernald would be pleased merely to arrest this man of violence and take him back to Catalina, there to be examined on the murder charge. But, if a fight there must be, let many witnesses be on hand to note that there was nothing but fair play! Thus spoke Pedrillo Oñate, and the crowd, intensely pleased, heard and rubbed its hands.

The challenge was wafted far and wide across the mountains. Somewhere, it would come to the ears of the proud Berners and certainly he would kill horses in his frantic haste to get home and defend his reputation.

The sheriff of that county rode in and interviewed Robert. He wanted to see the license by which Robert ventured to take the law into his own hands, and the commission from Minter was then shown.

Said the sheriff: "I've heard of gents laying traps but I never heard of anybody using himself for bait!"

That saying was repeated far and wide. Robert Fernald

had laid a trap, and then had used himself for bait. He had established himself in the home town of the gunman; and there with an open taunt was drawing Mr. Berners back to him.

Men waited with held breath until the inevitable word came across the ridges that Berners was on his way, riding night and day, never resting, burning with fury, and swearing that he would blast Robert Fernald from the face of the earth!

24

When this great news was heard, then the tidings were flashed to all parts of the neighboring countryside. Were there men who desired to be witness of the gun fight of the ages? Then let them appear in the town of Last Buffalo, for there the great battle was bound to take place.

The hotel overflowed. And on all sides, people were asking for a glimpse of Robert Fernald.

He was rarely to be seen. He remained much in his room. In the early mornings and in the late evenings he walked out from the hotel by the back way and went into the woods. There they heard him shooting patiently, industriously. Afterward, people went out to find the targets at which he had aimed, but according to the Mexican, the bull's-eyes which his master attempted were never larger than the mere twigs of trees!

For Pedrillo had no intention of allowing the fame of his master to diminish up to the very day of the fight.

As for the battle itself, Pedrillo knew its result be-
forehand. Robert Fernald was a brave man and a good shot
and a quick one; but Laurence Berners was a ruffian who
had lived by the gun all these years. How could Robert be
expected to stand before him?

For all the preparations that were made, the coming of
Berners was a good deal of a surprise. A horse clattered to a
halt outside the saloon of Chick Murphy. The swinging
doors were thrust open, and there entered a squat, wide-
shouldered man, with a lower jaw thrust prominently forward.

It was Laurence Berners, hollow-eyed and haggard from
the fury of his long ride.

"Is the rat here?" asked Berners slowly. And he looked
up and down the barroom.

There was a general movement through that crowd.
Each man stepped back a little toward the wall, as though
hoping that some other neighbor might come under the
keen scrutiny of the man of war.

No, Robert Fernald was not there. But Pedrillo was
there. The fat Mexican was there, and on his lips the name
of his master had barely died away.

"There's Fernald's man," said the bartender, who on this
eve was Chick himself.

Mr. Berners strode down the barroom and confronted
the Mexican.

Two things saved the face of Pedrillo. One was the color
of his skin, which prevented his pallor from being immediately noticeable. The other was the memory that he
had only one hand, and that Westerners would not allow a
bully to pick on a cripple.

So Pedrillo raised his head high and waved his one hand
with a smile.

"Good evening to you, Señor Berners," said he. "I might
say that I'm glad to see you here, señor. But I cannot. Were

I your friend, I'd be wishing you any other place in the world!"

"You greasy hound," said Mr. Berners, thrusting his face within an inch of the face of Pedrillo, "where's the skunk, your master?"

"Do you mean Señor Fernald?"

"I mean the fool kid that's been talking big in Last Buffalo. And these saps—these flatheads, these wall-eyed suckers, that've stood around and believed him! Why, I'm gonna eat that kid alive. But first of all, I'm gonna show him off before the whole doggone town! Where's Fernald, I say?"

Pedrillo was frightened. But he had all the instinct of an actor. Now he made the most of his great moment.

"Look here," said Berners, "are you talkin', or do I have to break you open and read your mind for myself?"

"Ah, señor," said Pedrillo, "I understand exactly why you are excited. You wish to meet my master. You wish to show that you are not afraid—but, señor, my master cannot meet you tonight."

"Ten thousand damnations," cried Berners, "is the yaller dog gonna—"

"There are two reasons," said Pedrillo, who as a matter of fact had received no instructions whatever from his employer.

"Give 'em," said Berners, "and I'll prove that neither of them is worth a cent."

The Mexican looked shrewdly at this man of war. It was not hard for him to see that Mr. Berners was keyed up to the point of finest execution. Let him fight now, and he would be more steel than human. He would have caught a lightning bolt in his naked hands and hurled it back at the sky.

"The first reason, señor," said Pedrillo, "is that my master does not like to fight with you. He knows that you are brave

125

and strong. But he has met many braver and stronger men. There is no glory to him for killing you. But if you insist on meeting him with weapons—"

"Why," shouted Berners, purple with fury, "I'm gonna—I'm gonna shoot him to bits, by degrees! Why, one killin' ain't good enough for what I'm gonna do to him!"

"Ah, well," said Pedrillo, affecting to sigh with regret. "You are brave, señor, and you are foolish, but my master has told me that he will not force you to fight. You have only to surrender your guns to me, and then promise—"

"Surrender my guns to you?" cried Berners, beside himself.

"Very well, then," said Oñate, with a graceful wave of his hand. "If you force my master to kill you, he must do so. But he will not take you tonight. He does not wish to have you at an advantage. He wishes to meet you when you are not tired from a long journey, but when you are rested and steady of nerves. Then he will gladly meet you!"

"You brown-faced rat!" called Berners. "All I'm gonna do is to find him and make him—"

"Furthermore," said Pedrillo, "My master prefers to meet you in the morning, when there is daylight. Lamplight or moonshine or sun, are all the same to him, but he does not wish to take any advantage of you!"

"I've come here a-bustin' and a-ragin'," said the warrior, "and I've had short sleeps and I've rode long hours, and now I find that sneak is gonna stay in a hole until tomorrow morning!"

"But," said Pedrillo, his imagination coming strongly to his rescue, "my master wants to make this as close to a fair fight as he can. Therefore he offers you any advantage which you may wish. He will let you have your gun in your hand, while his remains in the holster until the signal for the shooting—"

"Advantage?" shouted Laurence Berners. "Have you

gents all gone crazy? D'you let a greaser talk about anybody givin' me a handicap in a fight?"

"Laurie," said Chick Murphy solemnly, "the Mexican ain't four-flushin' or bluffin'. We've seen this guy, Fernald. We've seen him work. You better take what you can get! You may be sorry, if you don't!"

"I'll be dead first," said Berners. "But what's this stuff about shootin' at a signal? I dunno nothin' about signals, but I'll hunt for your boss in the morning, Mexican, and when I find him, I'll send him to another world. You go tell him that!"

Pedrillo was very glad to leave the saloon. He wanted to get to his master before Robert heard the report that his enemy had reached the town and started to meet him.

And, in fact, he got to Fernald's room at the very moment that Robert was clapping on a hat, preparatory to leaving the hotel.

Pedrillo told him everything, making the most of what he had seen and what he had heard and said.

"You do not wish to kill Berners by night," said Pedrillo with a grin. "You wish to give him the advantage of daylight—"

"Advantage," gasped Robert. "But he sees as well as I do, I suppose."

"You sent me to tell him that candlelight or starlight were all the same to you; but you would let him have the sunshine to die by."

"Pedrillo! You have been boasting to him in my name!"

"No, señor!"

"If you have, I'll make you—"

"No, no, señor, but I knew that you would not want to fight a nervous, tired man—"

"Ah, that is true, of course," said Robert. "Poor Pedrillo, I have been suspecting you, and all the time, you have been thinking only of my honor."

127

This made the Mexican easy.

"And your life," said Pedrillo, but he said it softly, to himself, for he knew that if Robert suspected that trickery had been used on his behalf he would be in despair. "At ten o'clock in the morning," added Pedrillo, "you are to kill Señor Berners!"

25

The dread of Pedrillo had been lest his master should balk at these arrangements which he had made with such care. But once he was sure that Robert would be docile, his pleasure and his confidence knew no end. He went from the room of Robert Fernald and called at the saloon where Mr. Berners was now drinking whisky in wholesale quantities and vowing terrible vengeance upon Fernald for the latter's insolence in daring to come to Berners' own city.

To him, Pedrillo said calmly: "Señor, my master bids me tell you that at ten o'clock in the morning he will wait for you on the veranda of the hotel. He begs you to have your gun in your hand at that time. He himself will step through the door onto the veranda at ten o'clock with his gun in its holster. Or, if you wish a greater advantage than this, Señor Fernald is willing to listen to any reasonable request."

"You fat-faced fool!" shouted the irate Berners. "Go back and tell him that I'll take a fair start with him and that I don't want a handicap from any man in the world!"

So said Berners, and glared around him expecting to meet with applause, but he saw that all eyes were looking steadily at the floor, as if they feared that their looks might be held against them on another day.

He stamped out of the saloon thinking that the entire world had gone mad. He took himself to the house of his mother, that cruel woman of iron, and there he fell into a bed and tried to sleep.

In the meantime, strange scenes went on in the saloon of Chick Murphy which was doing all the business this evening for the good reason that Pedrillo Oñate saw fit to give the place his patronage. And there Pedrillo heard the odds offered and taken on the probable outcome of the fight the next morning.

Two to one was freely offered upon Fernald. Three to one was asked and given. Four and five to one were finally the closing bets, and at this figure Pedrillo Oñate did not scruple to put down his money, which consisted of a scanty fifteen dollars.

All the city was stirring by sun-up. Ten o'clock was far away, but there were choice places to be gained, and the townsmen wished to have them. And so a murmuring, whispering, eager throng gathered and filled the veranda, crowded the doors and the windows of the houses just across the street, and packed the windows of the hotel that opened upon the porch.

Nine o'clock rang clear and loud by the big clock within the hotel hall.

Shortly afterward, there was a ripple of interest up and down the town.

Berners had left his house and was seen sauntering slowly down the exact center of the street. He carried a rifle in his hands, at the ready, and two heavy revolvers were in his belt. In this fashion he advanced to the steps of the hotel. There Berners took stock of the people who were crowded in waiting—and made a single gesture with the gun.

"Get out of this!" he commanded.

129

At once the veranda was vacated. Berners sat with his rifle across his knees in a chair which faced the door of the hotel.

Presently he seemed to feel that a rifle was not just the weapon for work at this range. He discarded it, picked out the two revolvers and sat on guard with a weapon in either hand.

Then he heard the voice of rumor, like a snake hissing in the crowd.

"Look! Berners is going to take his handicap! He's going to have his guns out!"

"You lie!" shouted Berners to that sneering comment, and forthwith jammed both guns back into their holsters.

He began to grow nervous. It was only half-past nine, and thirty mortal minutes lay between him and the appointed moment. He made a cigarette; but halfway through the making a spasm of terror seized him, for he thought he saw a movement among the shadows inside the door of the hotel. Instantly the cigarette dropped from his hand, and he snatched out both his guns.

"His nerve's gone!" said the whisper in the crowd.

Berners heard that whisper also. And he half believed it. This was far different from galloping into a town with a gun smoking from either hand. This was different from the rage and sudden challenge such as comes before a barroom brawl.

Then, within the hall of the hotel, the loud-voiced clock began chiming the hour of ten.

Berners leaned forward in this chair, tense, sick, white about the lips; and at the same time he heard a deep voice saying: "Here comes the finish of Berners!"

He wanted to turn—he was fiendishly tempted to whirl about and drive a bullet through the heart of that prophet. It would have done him good to ease himself in that way. It would have prepared him for the fight to come!

26

At the first chime of the clock, Robert rose, fumbled inside his coat to make sure that his automatic was held easily, and then started slowly toward the door of the building. Outside, where the sun glared like the blast of a furnace, death lay for him, perhaps. And yet he suddenly knew that he would not have wished himself in any other place. Cavaselle had been right. Danger was what he loved!

It made him tremble, but it made him coldly, terribly ecstatic. He shuddered with a fierce joy. He tried to make his face grave and thought that he had succeeded, but in spite of himself a faint smile was showing at the corners of his mouth. When he walked out, people watching gasped when they saw that smile.

"He's happy! He likes it! He ain't hardly human!"

He heard them keenly, and understood. Perhaps they were right! He heard everything. Every breath in the crowd, so it seemed—even the rustling of the clothes of the people who waited, crowded around the veranda.

Then, lightly, as the clock struck its last chime, he stepped through the doorway onto the veranda. Not straight out, but with a catlike stride to the side that brought him around the corner of the door and into the open.

As he stepped, he saw that Berners had changed his mind once more. With the first chime of the clock, he had jerked out both his guns again; and at the first glimpse of Robert, he tipped up the muzzles and sent a pair of balls humming through the doorway which Robert had stepped into and out of. One of those balls literally fanned his face.

So swiftly and completely was Robert seeing all things now, that he noticed the twitching of the gunman's body, and the manner in which he had half-risen from his chair like a jockey in his stirrups, riding a terrible finish. Death was the penalty for not winning this race of theirs!

To those who watched, it seemed that Robert moved like lightning. That one short step into the doorway, that swift glide to the side, and then a gun glinted in his hand and a spurt of fire came from its muzzle.

Berners lurched backward, floundered over the chair in which he had been sitting and waiting, and with a loud cry toppled upon the floor of the veranda. And as he sprawled there, Robert leaned above him and laid the mouth of his pistol in the hollow of Berners' throat.

It was not a very severe wound. The bullet had driven through Berner's shoulder, and the weight of the blow had staggered him.

However, he soon lay in bed, staring at Robert Fernald who sat beside him, while Pedrillo Oñate was in the saloon of Chick Murphy explaining: "He didn't want to kill Berners. He wanted to keep him alive to talk at the trial! Of course, that was what he wanted."

Now, in the room beside the bed of the wounded man, Fernald was saying: "You ride south with me to Catalina as soon as this wound is well, Berners."

"And what'll I do when I get south?"

"Tell the court what you have done."

"And you'll take me?"

"I'd never trust you to the hands of any other man to guard or bring you there!"

Berners closed his eyes. He was seeing in a vivid flash of imagination the picture of himself, the once terrible and feared Berners, riding tamely into Catalina at the side of his captor, the girl-faced, pink-cheeked Robert Fernald! And it was worse than the bitterest death to the gunman.

"Suppose that I got nothing to tell the court?"

"Let the court do the judging, Berners."

"Fernald, suppose that I was to *confess!* Would you take that confession along—and leave me here to take my own chances of escaping?"

"And why not?" said Robert.

It was a neat and brief confession:

I went to see Lovat at his own invite. He wanted me to take a hand in a crooked deal, to take the job on that Tom Gill had had before me, of running cattle out of Larkin Valley. Because Lovat wanted a chance to buy that valley cheap and he wanted to make it too hot to hold the girl that runs it now. He wrangled about terms. Finally, we got hot. He cursed me. He even went for a gun. Then I killed him.   LAURENCE BERNERS.

Robert Fernald took the precious document and rode south, with Pedrillo grunting on mule-back behind him.

Two days later a double item of news appeared in the papers. The silversmith, Bede, had been freed from prison; and the confessed murderer, Berners, most daringly had escaped from his guards in Last Buffalo in spite of his wound. Now he was at large and thought to be drifting north toward Canada. "All is well, and the honest man is saved," sighed Robert.

But that same night, Fernald sat with Tim Cavaselle and Chollie and Austin Bede in the house of the latter—in the kitchen, for only the kitchen fire could keep them warm, the mountain night had turned out so cold. And he said: "I have to ride on a long journey to Larkin Valley. I only wish to ask one question: Why were you cleaning a gun in the kitchen, Miss Bede, the night that Mr. Lovat was killed?"

Miss Bede turned white. "Are you the devil?" she cried.

"Young man, I'll tell you what she was doing!" said Austin Bede.

"No, no, Dad!" cried the girl.

133

"I'll tell him," persisted the silversmith. "She was cleaning the gun with which I had just shot Lovat. And I would shoot him again if I had the chance given me again. The fight between us was an old one, Mr. Fernald. It was for my wife first of all, and I won. He came back. It was for Chollie, then, and I thought his money was going to win. I went to his room. We fought it out man to man. But my stiff old arm was faster than his. I killed him!"

Robert choked, gasped, stared.

"And the jewels?" he murmured.

"I don't know what became of them," said Bede, "unless it was that Berners may have got into the room and stolen them immediately after the shot was fired."

"But the money you had?" asked Robert.

"Honest money," said Bede. "I'd saved it to let my girl afford to marry an honest man. But she made me spend it on my creditors. So there's the story, Fernald. Now you can call for the sheriff if you wish."

But Robert had no such wish.

He stumbled out into the night. He felt very hot in the face. But, after all, he was not sure that he had been a fool. Only, he knew that human nature was far too bewildering for him ever to understand it in the slightest. Now Larkin Valley lay ahead of him. What would he find there that was not a human mask, hiding the reality of the soul?

27

Pat McGuire is the greatest man in Crawfordville, the boldest, most famous spirit; and in his saloon all the celebrated people of the range appear; but no one in that saloon catches the eye so clearly and quickly as does Pedrillo Oñate.

Standing there at the far end of the bar, he glows like a beautifully feathered tropical bird. And indeed, he is a mass of color and of metal. His lofty sombrero is banded around with heavy golden ornaments. It makes one's forehead burn even to think of enduring such a weight in such weather as this. He wears a jacket of yellow deerskin, threaded and chased with golden thread, and embossed with massy silver. His boots shine a dull, mahogany-red glow, his trousers are ornamented with solid silver conchos, and the holsters which support his two guns—what use has a one-armed man for two guns?—are of the purest white leather worked and chased with gold!

His fat cheeks glisten as though they had been coated with polish and rubbed hard. His black eyes seem blacker and brighter. And he smiles continually, out of the greatness of his sense of well-being.

He drinks tequila, slowly, sipping the white fire drop by drop, spending half an hour over a single glass. Others swallow whisky with a gulp before they are crowded from their places by thirstier drinkers. But Pedrillo takes his time, leaning his one elbow on the bar, at ease, cool, smiling, content. His ears are busy listening to a hundred broken conversations, piecing them together, making of them

135

the groundwork upon which he will rear a fabric of inventions later on.

Yet the attitude of Pedrillo is not entirely that of a man who listens idly. In it there is something more narrowly attentive. There is an air of eagerness and an air of patient expectation combined. Study the face of a fisherman, and you will see the same expression.

For what does he wait there? For what is he fishing, this transfigured and radiant Oñate?

Presently, out of the crowd comes a fellow dressed like any cowpuncher; a man of middle age, with fat jowls, a hawk nose, and eyes glittering with a wonderful brightness. Even a dog could have guessed that this was a man of evil. But Oñate did not seem to care. He noted the approach of the other from the corner of his eye, and pretended to heed the newcomer not at all. But that was not the truth. His expectant attitude had ceased. His expression had changed. Oñate now has a fierce glitter in his eye, a fierce but contented glitter, so that he looks no longer like the merely idle fisher. Now he has something on the hook.

Once, twice, and again the man of the hook nose and the bright eyes looks earnestly at Oñate. Then he comes closer. He steps into the little enchanted clearing which surrounds the Mexican. He waits quietly, his eyes attentive. Still Pedrillo pays no heed!

And, all the time, like a hawk watching a sparrow, Pedrillo is watching this newcomer, judging him, regarding especially the size of a diamond ring upon his finger.

At length, the stranger steps briskly up to the bar and looks Pedrillo in the eye.

"You're Pedrillo Oñate, I guess," says he.

"I am," says Pedrillo.

"Well, then," says the stranger, "I think we can do business together. And back yonder is a little empty room where we can talk. Come along!"

When he had said this, he turned on his heel and walked

straight toward the little back room which he had desig-
nated. Pedrillo stared. He wanted to follow, because he felt
that this interview might be much to his advantage. But on
the other hand, he did not like the assured manner in
which this stranger led the way, confident that Pedrillo
would follow. It angered Oñate. It made him frown. But
curiosity was stronger than resentment, and presently he
walked, scowling, on the heels of the stranger and into the
little back room.

How strange it was to see the completeness with which
all diffidence vanished from the manner of the unknown!
He sat at his ease among the shadows of the farthest corner,
and rolled a cigarette. This he lighted, and through the
dimness and the smoke which he puffed forth, he examined
Pedrillo closely—without malice but without friendship.

"Oñate," said he suddenly to the frowning Mexican, "do
you know me?"

"No."

"I'm Sim Burgess of the Big Bend. Does that help you?"

"No," said Pedrillo, growing more and more haughty.

"Very well," said Sim Burgess, "I'll tell you a little bit
about myself. You'll find it pretty interesting. I've got a big
piece of land staked out down in that part of the world. Me
and a partner staked it out, stocked it with cattle, and
worked it into a going ranch. We worked like brothers.
He's my heir, and I'm his heir. We wrote out that one will
and we filed it away in a bank. Neither of us could change
it. Neither of us could take that will out of the bank vault
without the permission of the other man. You understand?
Now, Pedrillo, we had a little falling out. No matter about
what. Each of us thought that the other fellow was wrong.
And so we had that falling out. He got more of the boys
behind him. I was run off the place. You understand? Well,
he gives me a pension but he won't let me come back. You
understand? I have to stay away and live like a dog on the
two or three thousand a year that he sends to me. Now,

Pedrillo, you can see where you come in. You get him shot for me, and I hand you a big wad of dough. Is that clear? Is that simple? You get him shot for me, and I get the ranch, because the double will will hand it to me. You get a big chunk of handy coin. Now, how does that sound to you?"

Pedrillo rolled a cigarette—it was a miracle to see how he manipulated the paper, the sack of tobacco and all, with one hand, rolling the cornucopia-shaped smoke with a single twist—and thrust it into his mouth. He lighted it. Through the smoke which he presently sent upwards in great exhalations, he studied the idea which had been presented to him.

"Your partner is Pete McCoy," said Pedrillo.

Sim Burgess nodded.

"McCoy is a grand fighting man."

"Yes."

"That makes the price high, señor."

"Of course. I understand that."

"And then, it is a big ranch, I think. I have heard about it."

"It's not so big as you've heard, maybe."

"You make fifteen thousand dollars a year on that place, señor."

"It's a lie," said the other, "we've never cleared more than twelve!"

Then he bit his lip, because by the smile of the Mexican he saw that he had been tricked into giving important statistics. "And that was our banner year; we've never had another like it," he added.

The smile of Oñate was radiant as before. "I think that we shall agree, señor," said he. "I never believe in a hard bargain. I know that people must live. They cannot be taxed too heavily. But still, this is a great affair. Suppose that we say twenty thousand dollars for this job, señor?"

Sim Burgess rose slowly from his chair, as one partly

startled, and partly dismayed. "Twenty thousand," said he at last. "Are you nutty?"

"Or fifteen thousand," said Pedrillo gently, seeing that he had overstepped himself a little.

"Oñate," said Mr. Burgess hotly, "I'll pay fifteen hundred for this job. Does it sound good to you?"

Pedrillo waved the unhappy idea away.

"Let us finish our drinks," said Pedrillo. "Let us talk business no longer."

Mr. Burgess lost some of his fury and began to argue; first he tapped off his points, forefinger on palm; then he smashed them off with a clenched fist.

"What's hard about it? A little trip. Just a fine little jog. Then you meet up with McCoy. He's got a temper strung on a hairtrigger. You touch him and he explodes. But of course he wouldn't have a chance against your man. And, well, Oñate, ain't it perfect for you? I know your Fernald. He's a sort of halfwit. Hunting for action and trying to do good, like something out of a kid's book. Well, he runs into this perfect setup for him. Ain't it easy? Here's me that has been kicked out of a partnership by a big brute of a gun fighter like McCoy. Why, what more could Fernald want if his tongue is hangin' out to do a good deed? You tell me, kid. You tell me, will you? I'll listen! You've got your spiel made up for you! Why, I could've gone straight to him and told him the sad story. I wouldn't 've had to pay a cent!"

"The way is open, señor," said Pedrillo with a wave of his fat brown hand. "You have still a good chance to speak to him."

Mr. Burgess hurled himself onto his chair and scowled. Twice he began to speak, and finally he said: "Aw, I understand. You queer any deal except the ones that you promote. Look here, Oñate, I'll raise the ante. I'll make it ten thousand flat."

"I split the difference with you," said the Mexican gra-

139

ciously. "I am not a robber. But one must live, señor. I split the difference and call the price twelve thousand five hundred dollars."

"All right," Burgess sighed. "But you've got a nerve with you! Twelve grand for—well, I'm the sucker! When do you start?"

"Before tomorrow morning. And now to bind the agreement, señor?"

"To bind the agreement? Here's five hundred, Oñate."

"Thank you," said Oñate, and, deliberately, he spread out the bills and counted them. "Correct," said he. "Five hundred and that diamond ring, señor?"

"This?" cried Burgess. "Oñate, I'd hate to tell you what kind of a shark you are. By heaven, I would! But the fact is—"

"Yes, señor?"

"Well, take it and be hanged!"

He tossed the ring on the table and Oñate picked it up between fat thumb and fat forefinger. It would not fit except on the little finger, and there he placed it; and turned his hand gently back and forth, admiring, it seemed, the deep wrinkles at the wrist.

"This will do very well," said the Mexican.

"Will it?" snarled Burgess. "Now you tell me, will you, what sort of surety *I* get that the job will be done?"

Oñate raised his eyes reluctantly from the brilliance of the jewel.

"Ah, señor," he murmured at length, "as for that, you have the word of a gentleman!"

So he said, and returned his attention to the ring; while Burgess rose and went slowly out into the broad, bright flare of the sun. Not until he had reached the outdoors did the full sting of the Mexican's last sentence enter his mind. He turned as if to go back, but again he altered his purpose and merely shrugged his shoulders, like a good gambler who had risked his last stake upon a long shot.

28

Oñate, ready to practice his skills as a liar, sat with his head in his hand, sighing profoundly.

"What is wrong, Pedrillo?" asked Robert.

"It is for the evil that I find in the world that I sigh, señor," says Pedrillo.

"That is true," replies Robert Fernald mournfully.

"But what would the señor say of a man good, sincere, brave, and honest, who becomes the partner of a villain, builds up a great ranch, loves his partner like a brother, so that he agrees to a mutual will in which each leaves all his property to the other, and then—alas, little father, I cannot tell you!"

"That is the picture of a good man, full of trust," says Robert, much moved. "Tell me more, Pedrillo!"

"Will you believe that there can be such a villain? Yet I tell you on my honor, the scoundrelly partner gathers the men of the ranch together, bribes them and fills their minds with poison, and then drives away the honest man! Think of this, señor! With bribery and treachery he corrupts the men of the ranch—they drive out the good man whose brains and whose money have made the ranch rich—"

"What is the name of this devil of a man, Pedrillo?"

"Señor Don Peter McCoy."

"I shall remember! Where can he be found?"

"In the Big Bend, señor."

"Would it not be a good work, Pedrillo, to find this cur and rid the world of him?"

"Ah, little father, think what you say! To risk your life—because he is a terrible fighter—"

"Is he?" says Robert Fernald softly. "Is he such a terrible man?"

"Ah, señor, the list of those he has slain—"

"He is a great man with guns, Pedrillo?"

"Ah, yes! If you were to stand against him, it would simply be death to you, señor!"

"A man may die only once," said Robert Fernald gravely, "and why not in a good cause?"

"What have I done?" cries Pedrillo, the cunning one. "No, little father, I never shall cease—"

"I have decided!" declared Robert Fernald firmly. "Learn where the ranch is to be found in the Big Bend. Then bring me word of it at once!"

"No, no! We now are on the way to Larkin Valley, where you long ago had promised to be—"

"I have made up my mind, Pedrillo. Nothing can change me! Who is the poor man who was driven away from his rights?"

"Señor Burgess. The world knows that he is an honorable man."

"Your word is enough for me. Hurry, Pedrillo. Find out everything. Let me know at once. Now go."

So, with seeming reluctance, Pedrillo was driven from the room. Once outside the door, he shrugged his shoulders and went smilingly down to the street where, at the first corner, he encountered Burgess.

"Greaser," said Sim Burgess, "what's been arranged?"

Pedrillo overlooked the insulting nickname.

"It is finished," said he, "except that the coffin for Señor McCoy has not been ordered. But you will attend to the burial, my friend?"

"You've got Fernald on the job?" asked Burgess, his eyes glittering with pleasure and excitement.

"He is eager to go. He burns when he thinks of the scoundrel McCoy!"

Burgess grinned, slowly and wickedly.

"Now, keep the kid under cover all the way to the Big Bend," said he. "Don't let him have too much air, for if you do, he'll hear something that'll poison his mind. He'll hear folks talking about McCoy, and damn me if ever you hear anything against him. He's got people hypnotized!"

"I shall take him," said Pedrillo, "by such ways that even the eagle hardly knows them. We shall not meet others by the trail I travel!"

Burgess grinned again.

"I dunno," said he, "but somehow I feel as if the ranch was in my pocket already. Tell me, Pedrillo, how it comes that your boss never sees the inside of a jail, the number of fights that he's been in?"

"There is a simple reason. He does not fire until the other man draws a gun. And he rarely kills. A shoulder or a hip is his target."

"Is it?" murmured Burgess. "But this is different. A wounded McCoy ain't a thing to me. It's a dead man that I want!"

"He is dead already," said Pedrillo. "And before we come to the ranch, Señor Fernald will wish for nothing in life except to kill this scoundrel!"

And he looked down to the glittering diamond upon his finger.

"If you was to double cross me," said Burgess, filled with a new emotion, "there wouldn't be nothin' in the world that would keep me from you, old-timer. I'd just nacherally have to hunt you down, even if you was to lay a trail clean around the world. You understand?"

"Nothing could be clearer. But you forget—my master never fails!"

Here they parted; and Burgess wandered slowly down

the street, hurrying a little through the patches of burning sun, and loitering through shadow. His mind was far in the future. Already he had the sense of great property. It was placed literally within the grip of his hands and he had only to close his fingers over it. And he flattered himself that even if he were not a miracle of industry like McCoy, at least he would be able to hire the proper people to run the place for him.

In the midst of these thoughts a voice hailed him, a voice straight out of the heart of his dream, and Burgess, with a start and a groan, whirled and blinked up at a tall, lean, brown-faced man who had reined a mustang to that side of the street.

"McCoy!" said Burgess. "Good Lord, what are you doing down here?"

"Why shouldn't I be here?" asked McCoy, stern and cold. "Now that I've seen you, I want to talk business with you."

"Come over here to the saloon," said Burgess.

"I don't want to talk to you over liquor," answered McCoy, with a certain amount of disdain. "I want to talk business, not old times."

"Then fire away."

"I want the ranch."

"That's a funny thing. So do I."

"There's a difference, though."

"I don't see it."

"I'll pay for what I want—and you'll only steal what you want!"

Burgess scowled, and said sullenly: "Look here, are you gunna stop here only to insult me, McCoy?"

"I don't want to insult you. I was simply showing you a difference. Now, Burgess, I want you to listen to some hard facts."

"Go ahead, then. I'll listen."

"I'll pay you fifty thousand for your share in the ranch."

"You will! And you makin' between twelve and fifty thousand a year—and every year more! You'll pay me fifty thousand?"

"Don't be a fool, Sim. I make that money by hard work."

"So could I. But you run me off of the ranch! What chance have I got to show you what I could do with the place?"

"You showed it long ago. The year that you worked it with me, we had a deficit. You spoiled everything that you tried."

"That's what you think. Simply because my way ain't yours!"

"The proof of the pudding is the eating. After you quit, I made the ranch pay; when you were there everything went to ruin. Now, Sim, I'm offering you a nice fat sum. Fifty thousand can bring you in three thousand a year, dead easy. Do you want it, or don't you?"

"Is three thousand half of twelve? No! You want to rob me, McCoy."

McCoy started to speak and again changed his mind.

He reined back his horse into the street.

"I've made you a proposition," he said, "and you can think it over for a while. I'm gunna be in town for a few days. You can find me and tell me what you want to do."

29

There was great haste in Sim Burgess now. He wanted to get to the Mexican at once so he hurried back to the hotel. There he was informed that Pedrillo had left the hotel, and that his master, Robert Fernald, was now in his room, having given orders to have his bill prepared for he was leaving at once.

All this was very well; but Sim Burgess wanted nothing less than the departure of these two for the Big Bend, now that their quarry was in the town. He went to the stables. Oñate was not there. He returned in a froth of impatience to the veranda of the hotel and sat down there to wait.

While he waited, he saw McCoy come out on the veranda, and stand tall and silent by the pillars near the steps. No one spoke to him. He was not a person to be lightly addressed.

Without moving, that statue of a man remained on watch. And now he had the reward of his patience, for a little cavalcade came riding down the street: three men and two women—three hardy cowpunchers with all the signs of their calling about them, and two women of whom the one rode like a true daughter of the West, with a fine, free, careless swing, and the other was elderly, and mounted on a sidesaddle on a long-limbed thoroughbred. Such a cavalcade would have drawn more than a passing glance in any city; in this little town it became the cynosure of all eyes, and Sim Burgess came to the edge of the veranda and watched the newcomers.

They halted at the hotel; two of the men took the horses, and the third, with the two women, entered the hostelry. Sim Burgess, and all the idlers near by, strolled casually in to hear what they could hear and see what they could see— particularly the face of the girl. For she was a black-eyed beauty with such a store of good spirits that she smiled continually.

The idlers and Sim Burgess heard her ask the proprietor if there were a guest in his hotel under the name of Robert Fernald.

"Robert Fernald is here, ma'am," said the proprietor. "I suppose you've heard a good deal about him?"

"I'll tell a man I've heard a good deal about him!" said the girl. "And I've ridden all the way from the mountains to see him."

All the way from the mountains—those enchanting, cool, blue heaps against the far-off sky! All that distance to see young Robert Fernald! The air suddenly tingled with the spice of romance and excitement. What could have brought her?

"Dan," she said to the big fellow who had been signing the register, "will you try to find Robert and bring him to our room? Come along, Aunt Harriet, will you?"

She and Aunt Harriet went up the stairs, and Dan followed them, guided by the fat proprietor who had huddled himself into a coat in order to do honor to these new guests. The room of Sim Burgess, by chance, stood next to that of Robert Fernald, who spent most of his time in his chamber; busy, rumor had it, with a book, or spending hours and hours in studious practice with his guns, drawing and pointing at a crack in the door, or at a nail head, or at a rift in the ceiling, and going through his maneuvers seated or standing, or walking to and fro and whirling to aim again.

How many had he struck down with bullets, how many had he turned into mortal foes—brothers or fathers or cousins or friends of his fallen men? Therefore he must spend these hours at practice with his weapons, and if he dared to relax or give over the work, then he would fall. Fall he must, sooner or later. So declared rumor; so announced tradition. For those who live by the gun must die by the gun. That is the law of the West!

Mr. Sim Burgess hurried up to his room, therefore, keen with curiosity to learn what was about to happen behind the paper-thin partition which separated his chamber from that of the gun fighter. He paused only to glance at the hotel register, and there he found inscribed the names of Harriet Atkinson, Daniel Parker, and Beatrice Larkin.

Beatrice Larkin! That linked up suddenly with the tradition which had to do with Robert Fernald. So many tales had been breathed across the desert of the wild exploits of this mild-faced youth that one grew to thinking of them rather as fancies than as facts. And here was a legend which seemed to have a body—that legend which told how Robert Fernald had gone to Larkin Valley and there had captured the notorious Tom Gill.

With this idea tucked away in his mind, Burgess reached his chamber. He did not enter it in a rush, for all his haste; but with a soft-footed ease, such that any casual passerby would have shrewdly suspected him of being a thief. Like a thief, then, he entered his own room, making not a sound. And there he took a chair and sat still as a mouse.

That done, it was easy enough for him to hear everything that passed in the adjoining room. The occupants barely had exchanged their first greetings, and Robert Fernald was saying that he was glad to see Dan Parker, and saying it in such a voice that it seemed as though he meant it.

"Now look here, old-timer," Parker was saying, "it's a queer fact that Larkin Valley can't get along without you. I've come down here to take you back."

"I'd like to go," said Robert Fernald. "And as a matter of fact, there's no other place in the world where I'd be half so glad to go. But just now I can't."

"You're tied down?"

"Yes."

"You couldn't tell me about it?" said Dan Parker at last, in an oddly dry voice.

"I can't, Dan. It's not a thing that I can talk about very well. I'm not held back by any promise. But the fact is—it's a very private affair."

Sim Burgess, listening, quaked in his boots. For if this mission to which he had inspired Robert Fernald should be known, his own life would probably be ended by the hands of a lynching party.

"This private affair—it means that you're going off on a death-trail, Fernald!"

Robert was silent.

"Of course it means that. But look here, old fellow. Miss Beatrice has come down here a long ways—"

"Is it possible!" cried Robert Fernald.

But before he could say more, there came a light tap at his door.

"Come in!" called Robert.

Then the door creaked, and a breath of silence followed, after which the eavesdropper heard Fernald say in a husky voice: "Miss Larkin, I'm so happy—I mean surprised—I mean—how do you do—and won't, won't you sit down—and—"

"Bobbie," said the voice of a girl, laughing, "you *are* the silliest child in the world. Sit down yourself. You look much more in need of support!"

30

"Bobbie," said the girl, "you're coming to Larkin Valley with me."

"I, Miss—I mean, Beatrice—I—of course it's a thousand times kind of you to ask me but the fact is—I have to do a little work—"

"For whom?"

"For a good and just man who has been deprived of—"

"Something by a villain?"

This crisp voice of the girl seemed to scatter the dreamy thoughts of Robert Fernald.

"The fact is, Beatrice," he added suddenly, "this is a terrible case of cruelty and ingratitude—"

"And you have to kill somebody, accordingly?" she asked.

"Ah, Beatrice, how can you ask me such a thing?"

"Because I've heard enough about the things that you've been doing. Knocking off ninety per cent of the stuff for gossip and lies, that leaves ten per cent. Strike out half of that as exaggeration, and substract another twenty-five per cent of the cases because they've been good ones—but there still remains a considerable list of murders at your door, Robert Fernald!"

"I've never heard of such a thing!" breathed Robert. "You accuse me of murdering—but that is a terrible word, Beatrice!"

"Robert Fernald, how many dead men lie at your door?"

"I—I don't know, Beatrice," said Robert faintly. "Very, very few, I hope and trust!"

"You hope and trust!" said the girl scornfully. "Well, I can tell you of a few. There was that poor fellow in El Paso, young Gregory, whom you shot down in the street. And there were the Tucker boys in Idaho, and Charlie and Brent Hotchkiss in Butte City, and Lambert and King and the old—"

"Don't!" said Robert.

A little silence followed this.

And then Robert Fernald added: "They were wicked men, Beatrice. And every one of them had more than a fair chance."

"What do you call a chance?" asked the girl. "You give them a chance to make the first move to their guns. But they are people who haven't nerves as keenly strung as yours. Their hands can't move as fast. And perhaps they have something to do other than practice with weapons all

150

day long. You say that you give them a chance; but I'll tell you, Bobbie, that to pit you against most men is like pitting a wolf against an ordinary dog. The dog may be bigger than the wolf, but he can't live ten seconds against the biting of a lobo. Bobbie, you've killed eleven men—and I make no count of the rumors which give you a lot more."

"Eleven villains!" cried Robert. "Really, you must grant that!"

"Who judged them villains?" asked the girl angrily.

"Why, every one knew—"

"Are you twelve men and a judge, all by yourself?" asked Beatrice Larkin. "What do people say about you now?"

"I don't know," asked Robert. "Will you tell me?"

"You bet I'll tell you! They say you're a professional gunman."

"No, no!"

"They say you make your living with your guns. When you've downed a man, you let his enemies make you a present—of a fine saddle—a bridle all covered with gold—a magnificent Mexican sombrero—a glorious diamond. You take those presents and then you say like a hypocrite, these things are much too fine and gay for me. I'm only a simple, quiet fellow. You sell those gifts as a matter of course—and you use the money for living. Tell me, Bobbie, if that isn't a fact?"

He looked helplessly at her.

"And that's blood-money," said the girl, fiercely.

"I never thought of it like that," said he.

"Of course you didn't. But isn't it the truth? Ask other people. Ask Dan, won't you?"

"I don't want to be in on this," protested Dan Parker.

"Don't back down, Dan," urged the girl. "Tell him straight from the shoulder."

"Why, then," said Parker, "I suppose there's a good deal in what you've been telling Fernald."

"They think that I'm just—a murderer?" cried Robert.

There was no direct answer to this, and it seemed that silence was a sufficient speech.

Finally the girl said: "I've come for you, and I'm going to have you, Bobbie. I'm going to start back for the ranch tomorrow morning, and I'm going to take you with me."

"I want to think a little—" began Robert.

"Go out and walk around the block. We'll wait for you right here," she replied.

Presently Sim Burgess heard Robert leave the adjoining room. His first impulse was to hurry after his man of the guns and hurry him out of town on the blood trail. But he was greatly tempted to remain where he was and hear whatever might be said between the girl and Parker.

"You bore down on him pretty hard," said Parker, after Fernald was gone.

All her surety seemed to have left her. She said in a trembling voice: "Do you think that we'll be able to get him, Dan? What do you think?"

"I dunno," replied Parker. "He's got something on his mind!"

"It's the Mexican who leads him around by the nose from one deviltry into another; and sooner or later Pedrillo will get him killed. I know it! We've got to take him with us, Dan," said Beatrice.

"But there's Larkin Valley as quiet as can be," said Dan Parker. "I dunno that you got any great need for a gunman like Fernald, Miss Beatrice."

"You silly man!" said she, and laughed a little—a very uneven, uncertain laugh.

"Is that the way of it?" murmured Parker's gruff voice.

"Of course it is," said she.

"Humph!" said Parker. "But I'll tell you this. You'd no sooner get married to him, than one of his old enemies would turn up ready to fight. You'd be a widow almost before you was a wife."

"I'll guard him like a handful of diamonds," replied Beatrice Larkin. "Hush! Here he comes!"

Robert came hastily back to the room. He spoke in a sharp, broken voice: "Beatrice, I want to go back with you. But I've given my word of honor to another man. I have to try to help him. And then—"

31

The instant that Sim Burgess made sure his gun fighter par excellence was so devoted to his word of honor, he, Sim, determined that he must prepare to have the blow struck before the iron was a single degree cooler. No matter what the pull of duty and honor might be to this deluded Fernald, Burgess had a great deal of trust in the power of a girl as beautiful as Beatrice Larkin to do as she pleased with almost any man.

That was the reason for the haste of Burgess. When he got into the lobby of the hotel, however, he had to pause.

A most notorious character had arrived in town: Tiger Brennan, famous for a thousand wild and brutal acts—Tiger Brennan and his coterie of trained assistants. Trained, in fact, by the hand of the master, so that they would be useful in the performance of any act of crime that might prove profitable. There had been a time when Brennan roamed the range alone, doing whatever his patron, the devil, put into his mind; but that old and careless period had ended, and Brennan had learned how to make crime earn something more than various terms in jail.

He stood there in the corner of the lobby, surrounded, as

always, by a crowd. The majority were more interested, idle spectators, and with a single glance Burgess could pick out the cohorts of Brennan from the rest. Three tall, straight, lean-faced, young men with restless eyes and sternly set mouths, they showed that their master had selected them with care and trained them with patience. How many crimes were committed by these same youngsters, men only could guess. They were not constantly busy. It was said that Brennan planned every job with the utmost care, and that he struck but once.

Nothing was too big for him to undertake. Nothing was too small, if his pride were enlisted in a difficult undertaking. It was said that he had robbed trains, banks, messengers, stages. But nothing could be proved. Hardly a year went by that did not find him on trial for some spectacular breaking of the law. But he always escaped. He had skillful lawyers who knew how to frame his cases for him. And so he went scot-free.

He looked his full age, now. An iron-gray man was he, close to fifty; without surplus flesh, active, wiry, and a little straighter and faster with a gun than ever before, men said.

Mr. Burgess paused and regarded the great man with a measure of awe and a measure of envy. There was hardly an achievement of Brennan's that Burgess would not gladly have made his own.

Shaking his head, and with a sigh of envy, he went out from the hotel to the open street. And he found Pedrillo where he expected to find him—in the saloon, at the farther end of the bar.

Burgess went straight up to him.

"Oñate," said he, "there's complete hell to pay!"

"Alas, señor, do not say so," said the fat Mexican, his good-natured self-satisfaction entirely unruffled. "What can be wrong where there is so much good liquor!"

"Do you remember Miss Beatrice Larkin?"

"The señorita?" said Oñate, shrugging his thick shoulders with such violence that his entire body shook. "Ah, yes! And what of her? She had a cruel, bright eye! It went through one like the blade of a knife, grazing the heart! What of her, señor?"

"She's come here for your master!"

The Mexican gaped.

"Holy Virgin!" he breathed, and hastily swallowed a glass of tequila.

"It's the truth," said Burgess. "And you know, now, that McCoy is here in town? But I tell you that unless you work very fast, the girl will get Fernald away before he's had a chance to fight with McCoy. If you love the money that I've promised you, start to work, and start pronto!"

Oñate clutched the edge of the bar. So doing, his eyes caught the large diamond of his new ring. It fascinated him, not like a jewel, but like a great watching eye. To Oñate it had become more than human, and he would have done almost anything in this world rather than lose possession of it.

"Stay for me here," he said at last. "I shall go get my little father and bring him here to talk with you. He must know you, señor, before he will do such a thing!"

So Burgess, with a rising hope in his heart, waited for the coming of the young killer; and when Fernald arrived, all three walked in the yard behind the saloon, a big stretch of ground, dotted with poplars.

There Burgess told his story of lies with all the conviction that he could summon. And there young Fernald listened with a grave air, shaking his head from time to time as he considered the villainy of which the prosecuted Burgess spoke.

"It is all as Pedrillo has told me!" said Robert at last. "A good man fallen into the hands of a villain! Let me know where to find this scoundrel, and I'll go to him at once!"

Burgess gripped Robert's hand and wrung it with a mighty pressure.

"He's in this town—in this hotel!" said Sim Burgess. "The devil that has brought him luck all his life has deserted him now. He's left the Big Bend and come up here. God bless you, Mr. Fernald, if you can help me!"

"Here?" asked Robert, his eyes gleaming with a light that robbed his face of its fresh boyishness. "Here at this hotel?"

And without another word, he turned on his heel and strode from the yard toward the building.

Burgess exchanged glances with Pedrillo, mopping his brow the while.

"It's done, señor," said Pedrillo, "and McCoy is a dead man this minute!"

Robert wandered into the lobby to make inquiries about his quarry, but he did not have to search far.

"Where's Mr. McCoy?" he asked.

"Settin' right out on the veranda now, sir," said the proprietor, and he rubbed his fat hands together and smiled upon Robert.

Yonder on the veranda sat a possible opponent, a dangerous fighter, a mature and crafty brain. Yonder was an evil man—he had the word of Pedrillo for it! And through the doorway, Robert stepped with a heart as light as the heart of a hawk when it sees game rising from the covert far beneath.

It was not that he was certain of victory. What he loved was the thrill of the encounter, the facing of death, and above all, the dreadful moment of pause which generally preceded the actual battle. Other men were unnerved by that instant. To Robert it was like wine, a thing to be tasted, and prolonged in the tasting!

Such was his spirit, then, as he stepped onto the veranda; and, as he came out, he saw his quarry at once, seated in a chair at the farther end of the porch, tilted back against the wall of the building, with a few idlers on either side of him.

McCoy was in the very act of counting out a thick little sheaf of bills into the hands of a gray-headed fellow beside

156

him. And the latter, as he stuffed the money into his wallet, looked up to Robert, who was approaching with a step as light and gay as the beating of his own heart.

"Here we are," said the gray-headed man. "You've just made your dicker in time!"

Robert stood before the chair of McCoy.

"You're Mr. McCoy, I believe?" said he, in his gentle voice, but with his eyes as cold and bright as the eyes of a hunting bird.

"I'm McCoy," said the lean man.

"My name is Robert Fernald. May I have a few words apart with you, sir?"

"Words?" asked McCoy dryly. "D'you mean words, or bullets?"

Robert started, and flushed. He could hardly believe his ears.

"Is that what you mean?" said McCoy. "Well, lad, this ain't my day to be murdered!"

Robert gave back a little. It was a stunning surprise to him. For he had figured to himself a little stroll with McCoy down the street, and during that stroll he would suddenly confront the evil rancher and tell him in plain words his judgment of his companion. That done, of course guns would flash at once. There would be scores of witnesses to see that it was a fair fight—and then—

It was a simple plan. It should have worked. But here was an odd matter! It was as though McCoy had listened to the interview which had just taken place in the back yard of the hotel! But no matter what McCoy thought, he had been written down for Robert as a bold and courageous scoundrel, and pride should have made him rise to accept any challenge from a single opponent.

Instead, he leaned back in his chair and regarded Robert with perfect calm.

"Mr. McCoy," said Robert, "I think that you've said something which requires a little explaining."

"Have I?" replied the rancher indifferently. "Well, you

tell him, partner. You got the right to tell him, I guess!"

He gestured to the gray-headed man beside him.

"All right. I'll talk," said the latter, regarding Robert with a curious interest, not entirely hostile. "Kid, you don't know me?"

"I don't," said Robert, more and more bewildered.

"I'm Brennan."

"You're Brennan!" cried Robert turning very pale. "You're Tiger Brennan!"

"That's me, kid."

"I'm glad to know you," said Robert, standing stiff and straight as a soldier.

He was beginning to tremble a little, too.

"And you have something to say to me—for Mr. McCoy?" he added.

"I have, youngster," said Brennan, who was beginning to smile. For he felt that he recognized these symptoms of fear. He had seen them many a time before like this. And the same smile appeared on the faces of the lean, grim young men who were seated upon either side of the criminal.

"I'm waiting, sir," said Robert Fernald, and suddenly he smiled in turn, a mere flash of expression rather than an actual smile, a glance of light, as it were; but it had a great effect upon Mr. Brennan, for suddenly he could see that what he had taken for fear was not fear at all, but really a tense, overmastering, soul-absorbing joy in danger.

It altered his own attitude at once.

"My lad," said Brennan, "you're here lookin' for trouble and wanting it real bad. But you ain't going to get the kind that you want. You want to make a show out of this here, and what would please you would be to have a stand-off fight with guns. But you ain't going to get the gun fight, kid. Not that way. There was a time," he added, "when I would've taken you on quick and finished you off, too. But my time is too doggone valuable and I got too many important things on my hands to waste myself scrapping now with every young fool that wants to get famous. Matter of fact, youngster, all that you'll get out of us is a killing. Here's me, and McCoy, and here's my three partners, all ready to turn loose at you. And if you so much as raise a finger, kid, we'll surely blow you to bits!"

He leaned forward a little as he said this, and Robert looked him full in the eye—then flashed a glance on either side.

McCoy remained at ease in his chair, smiling faintly with satisfaction. The three young men were leaning forward a little, tense and quivering, like eager hounds straining at the leash. There was not the slightest doubt that they would be at him the instant he made a dangerous move.

And then a terrible temptation took Robert by the throat. There were five of them, to be sure, and they were all fighting men celebrated for their skill with weapons. McCoy and Brennan were known; and these three young disciples of the latter were doubtless experts with weapons of all kinds. Yet suppose that he should whip out two guns and plant two bullets—that would finish one pair out of the five. Then fall for the floor, shooting as he fell; and, with a little luck—because certainly these men would not be expecting such a frontal assault against such odds—why, if he were to do such a deed as this, he would become an historic figure—

That wild temptation stung the heart of Robert; and who can tell what he would have done, had not the hard, cold voice of McCoy cut in on him: "Don't do it, kid. You might get famous. But you'd get dead, too."

Robert straightened with a long, soft sigh.

"Brennan—and the rest of you," said he, "I'd like to know what is the meaning of all this!"

"I can tell you, sonny!" answered McCoy. "I've bought and paid for protection, and I've got it. You can go back to the dog that hired you and tell him that his medicine is no good. He's out of this here. He's tried to double cross me in every other possible way, and he's failed. Now he'll fail again. And he'll always fail. Because I've got his number, Fernald. He came high when he got you. But I came higher when I got Brennan."

And he chuckled a little, with a deep inner content.

Robert, quite baffled, went slowly away; and twice he paused to look back at the group on the veranda.

Instantly one of those tall, athletic youths who were with Brennan stood up.

"Where you gunna go, Charlie?" asked Brennan.

"Gunna take a lil' stroll," said the other.

He was a mighty man, slender about the waist, herculean around the shoulders and in the length and weight of his arms. And he stared earnestly in the direction of the hotel entrance through which Robert had just disappeared.

"Sit down, Dashwood!" said the master.

Dashwood hesitated, frowned, and then obeyed. But he was very restless, shifting back and forth in his chair as though he were terribly ill at ease.

"You want to take him by the throat, Charlie, don't you?" and Brennan grinned.

"And why not? The little runt!" muttered young Mr. Dashwood.

"It don't take a strong man to pull a gun," said Brennan wisely. "What good would all of your beef be against Fernald?"

"Have I got nothing but beef?" asked the youth quickly, and he turned his bold, bright eyes upon his master.

"You've got something else," admitted Brennan, "and you're gunna get still more, in time. But you ain't up to Fernald, just yet!"

"The proof of the pudding is in the eating," observed this sullen youth.

"Exactly. And though you've done a good deal of eating, kid, don't you get away with the idea that you can't be et in your turn. And that pink-cheeked kid is just the baby to turn the trick!"

"I don't see it," muttered Dashwood.

"Look here, Charlie, you're a brave kid. But would you tackle five men like the bunch of us here?"

"Well, no," said Dashwood. "I ain't that much of a flathead, I hope!"

"Of course you ain't. Well, lemme give you an idea about Fernald and the kind of a gent that he is. When he was standin' here, he wanted terrible bad to get at you and the rest of us. When I talked big over him, he come within an ace of letting drive at the bunch of us!"

"Him?" grunted Dashwood. "He was scared white!"

"He was white with wanting to tear us to pieces. That was all. Don't make no mistake, Charlie. You can't read men, yet. You need more training! Ask McCoy if the kid wasn't on edge to jump the whole gang of us?"

"I was never closer to dying," said McCoy calmly and judicially. "I knew that he would get you, Brennan, and me, with his first pair of shots. Maybe your boys would shoot him to bits afterwards, but the pair of us would've gone down first. That was why I spoke. I wanted to break the spell. And when he paused a bit, walkin' away from us, why, he was sayin' to himself: 'Ain't there a chance? If I was to turn back, ain't there a chance that I could kill the whole bunch of them by fast shooting?' That was the way that he was working things out in his head. And maybe he could. Anyway, it threw a chill into me."

Charlie Dashwood lost all of his restlessness and even shuddered a little, as a man will do when he has had a narrow escape.

And Brennan said at last: "I've seen 'em big and I've seen 'em small. I've seen 'em that fought for money, and I've seen 'em that fought for fame; but I've never seen one before that loved guns for the sake of the death that was inside of them! McCoy, I took on this here job too cheap!"

32

When Robert Fernald got back to his room, he fell into a quandary which lasted him all the rest of that day and kept him awake most of the night. He had only one visitor during this time, and the visitor was Dan Parker, who strode into the room and sat down on the end of the table.

He found Robert pacing restlessly back and forth, sometimes fidgeting at the window which looked onto the street, and again hurrying up and down the room as though in search of something he had lost.

"Bob, old fellow," said the ranch foreman, "tell me the straight of it. Are you coming back with us now?"

"Coming back?" snapped Robert, grown irritable.

"That's what I said."

"How can I come back, Dan? I've given my word to—"

"To kill McCoy?"

Robert gaped.

"The whole town knows about it," explained Parker.

"How?"

"You can't walk up to five men and ask for trouble without having the news spread around, Bob. But what makes the rest of us wonder is this: How'd you ever get mixed up in any job on the side of a gent like Burgess?"

"And what's wrong with him?"

"Why, he's a bad egg, that's all."

"You're generally right," said Robert, "but the fact is that you're completely out in this case, Dan. McCoy is a villain. And Burgess is the man he's wronged."

"Who told you that?"

"I had it from Burgess himself!"

Parker bit his lip. He wanted to scoff at this testimony, but he knew something about the childlike simplicity of Robert Fernald, and therefore he held his tongue.

"Had it from anybody else?" he asked.

"Yes, from Pedrillo."

"Oñate!" burst out Parker. "I knew he was at the bottom of the whole idiotic business!"

"Ah?" breathed Robert, and raised his head, a cold light in his eyes.

Dan Parker scowled at him.

"I know what you mean," said he. "You want to pick a fight even with me, Bob. But you can't. Because I'm not fighting you, you see. Suicide ain't my line. I get excitement other ways. But Oñate—the fat pig—the fat snake, I ought to call him! Why, Bob, you're letting him lead you around by the nose for his own profit!"

"Profit, Dan? Pedrillo's profit?"

"Who else? Why, Pedrillo is simply making a gold mine out of you."

"Ah, there in the very beginning you're all wrong! As a matter of fact, it's a wonderful thing that although Pedrillo has worked for me all this time, I simply can't make him take money!"

"Bob, you make me want to curse! As a matter of fact, the brown-faced swine is simply taking a commission for every job that he gets you to do!"

"Job?"

"Who worked you into this case of Burgess against McCoy? It was Oñate. And look back and you'll find that he's led you into the other fights that you've been having. Somebody profits out of those fights. Who? Why, Oñate, of course! His commission is what makes him rich."

Robert merely shook his head.

"I don't want to have my faith in him broken," said Robert. "In the first place, I know that it can't be. In the

163

second place, I don't like to have you try. Pedrillo is all right. You can't fool me about him, Dan, no matter what wrong impression you may have on the subject!"

Fernald said this with such emotion that Parker pursued the subject no further but left the room and went to a certain earnest and resolute young lady who was waiting to get a report.

Seeds of suspicion had been planted in the mind of Robert Fernald, however. He might deny that they had touched fertile soil. And, if they sprouted, he might hoe them up resolutely.

So the sway of Pedrillo Oñate was seriously threatened, though the danger might not come to a head for a long time. And Robert was left alone with increasingly serious thoughts, pacing back and forth in his room, and finally throwing himself face downward on his bed.

The sun was not up when trouble returned to Robert Fernald; the gray light filled his room when he was wakened next morning, and again it was by the entrance of big Dan Parker who was in a fury, cursing at every step he took.

"What's wrong?" asked Robert.

"Wrong? Everything's wrong! Miss Beatrice and her aunt are gone—spirited away—flown—and no trace of them left behind!"

Robert sat up in bed and stared.

"It doesn't seem possible!" said he.

"Don't tell me what seems possible or don't; I tell you what's happened. They told me to wake them just before daylight so's they could get a flying start this morning on the trail back to the ranch. I went and rapped at their door. No answer. I banged loud—no answer. I pushed the door open. By heaven, the lock of it was broken—it had been forced! There I found everying in disorder. And no sign of the pair of them. I ran downstairs to the stable. And there I found that their horses were gone. The stable boy was drunk, didn't know a thing. And Fernald, your man Pedrillo probably has had a hand in some dirty plot—"

He raged out these words in a shapeless jumble, so that Robert barely could make out his meaning. But when he did understand, he swung to the floor and stood up. He began to dress with frantic haste.

Pedrillo, who slept on a cot at the other side of the room, was likewise dressed, accomplishing his work with wonderful agility, considering his single hand.

Parker turned savagely upon the Mexican.

"He's behind it, Bob," he cried "You'll find out that Oñate had his hand in the thing!"

"You talk like a madman, Dan!" exclaimed Robert.

"Señor Parker," shouted Pedrillo, writhing with emotion, "I swear—I vow—I give my honor!"

"Your honor!" sneered the big foreman. "You ain't got none!"

"There's nothing gained by abusing Pedrillo," broke in Robert. "Have you raised the town? Have you sent for the sheriff—"

"What good will that do? We need to start and ride!" said Dan Parker. "Will you come with me, Fernald?"

"Alas, señor," said Pedrillo in haste, "you have given your word to—"

"To what?" broke in Dan Parker. "To kill McCoy? Is that what you mean, Oñate? Bob, that is proof of what I told you. The scoundrel is urging you on into an—"

"I've given my word," said Robert earnestly, "but I'll redeem it later without fail. What's the life of McCoy compared to the happiness of Beatrice Larkin? Dan, let's get to our horses—Pedrillo, raise the town—call out every one!"

Pedrillo, with a deep groan, went from the room, while Parker said: "We'll take a last look in their room—there may be some sort of clue—"

Into the deserted room of the two women they stormed, and almost at once Robert saw the thing that, in their hearts, they half expected. It was pinned against the rough wall with a splinter, a piece of paper that fluttered in the wind of their coming. Robert caught it from its place and found that it was covered with a roughly made writing.

Bring ten thousand to the foot of Crystal Mountain a week from today. They won't be harmed.

"Kidnaping!" breathed Robert, growing very sick.

He even had to steady himself by resting a hand against the broad shoulder of Dan Parker, who had snatched the paper from the limp fingers of Robert and was busy reading it in turn.

"I knew it!" groaned Parker. "I guessed it with the first look. Lord, what'll we do?"

"Start now for our horses—and then ride with the devil behind us!" said Robert through his teeth. "Are you ready, Dan?"

"Ready, lad. Yes, yes!"

Shoulder to shoulder they rushed down the stairs.

"Who could have done it, Dan?"

"Brennan? Why not Brennan? Isn't he the man for such a job as this? Would any one else have dared?"

"No one else would have dared!" shouted Parker suddenly. "Here's Brennan's room. Try him here—"

They beat at the door. It was locked, and silence answered them. Parker did not hesitate. One thrust of his powerful shoulder cast the door wide, and he lurched into the chamber. A glance was all they needed. The room was quite empty of any man or even blanket-roll; and the bed had not been slept in.

"God help us! God help us!" grasped Robert. "Hurry, Dan!"

The house was rising, now. Men were stumbling out of their rooms, most of them with naked guns in their hands, for in the distance there was the dreadful voice of Oñate, howling like a wolf. Swarms of men rose up around them, saddling horses, and making ready with much noise to take up the trail.

What trail? And where could it lead? Toward Crystal Mountain?

In five minutes groups of restless riders were sweeping this way and that around the village, cutting for sign in frantic haste, and finding nothing.

But this much was known. With two women, Brennan and his three companions had disappeared; and it did not need much forethought to connect the disappearance of the one with the disappearance of the other.

Robert and Parker, riding together, kept away from the other searchers until the snorting mule of Pedrillo brought that matchless trailer up with them. He had saddled as fast as he could to follow them, not because he wanted to be in on the work, but, no doubt, because he dreaded to be left behind in the village where McCoy could get at him—to say nothing of Sim Burgess, who would be wanting certain sums in cash and a jewel of value refunded.

So Oñate joined them; and, being with them, he could hardly help but use his rare talents. Put pencil and paper before an artist and a drawing must result. So it was with Pedrillo on the trail. He could not help but hunt, and it seemed that he could hardly help but find.

The wind of the night apparently had wiped out all traces, but on a stretch of firm ground beyond a draw, Pedrillo found what he wanted—the prints of the hoofs of six horses.

"We have a long hunt before us," said Pedrillo. "They left when it was still quite dark, and they were riding hard."

"How do you tell that, Pedrillo?"

"You see the distance that the horses were striding? That shows the speed of their gallop. And notice how close two of them came to that tree. They must have had to duck the branches. If it had been daylight, they would have swung wide.

"I'll call in a dozen of the best men," went on Pedrillo. "We'll need all their help if—"

"Wait for nothing," urged Dan Parker with much resolution. "Twelve men can't keep pace with six. And I saw Brennan's horses. He's mounted for a race!"

"You two against four?" cried Pedrillo, gaping.

"Are you willing?" Parker turned to Robert.

"Ready and willing," said Fernald. "Go on, Pedrillo! Hunt down this trail as you never hunted before!"

And he spoke to his pinto, and that hardy and beautiful little horse swung into a reaching gallop that consumed the ground as easily as the canter of a greyhound. They headed straight across the desert. The town dropped out of sight behind them. In silence they rode. The heat began to drop heavily from the heavens and wash back to them from the glowing surface of the sands. The surface grew yielding. They had to slow to a walk, and there is nothing so disheartening as a chase continued at a walk! The sand slushed softly around the feet of the horses; the stirrup leathers creaked; the horses puffed and snorted the blow-sand from their nostrils; they were proceeding rather like a plow team than a fleet-footed posse.

Then the Mexican said: "Listen to me, señors. You say that Señor Brennan has done this thing for ten thousand dollars. It is not possible!"

"Tell us why, Pedrillo."

"Señor Brennan has many men working for him. He cannot afford to waste his time on small game. And ten thousand is not much to him. Besides, this is not the sort of thing that he does. Here he has shown his hand openly. But he is as secret as a fox."

"The whole world knows that he has done this thing,"

said Dan Parker, scoffingly. "You have the facts in front of you, Pedrillo. How will you dodge them?"

"He seems to have stolen the two ladies," said Pedrillo, "and yet he cannot have done it. He has stolen them and yet he has not stolen them. And if this seems like madness, wait a little while, and you will see!"

33

A day passed, and another. They were days of scorching heat, endless labor. Again and again the trail was blotted out before their eyes. Nothing but the incredible skill of the Mexican was able to recover it, so it seemed.

Dan Parker was both cheerful and resolute. Robert Fernald was as a man devoured by a terrible fear. His face grew drawn. He stared constantly at the wavering heat lines along the horizon. But both Parker and Fernald were comparatively silent whereas the tongue of Pedrillo Oñate rarely ceased wagging.

"I am the eyes," said Pedrillo, "and I see the way into danger, and yet I cannot help going into the cave. There we shall be torn to pieces. What are two men against four? Four such men! I saw them. Like four mountatin lions. You are no more than mountain sheep. You will be cut to pieces. Afterward, they will strip me and turn me out to starve or let the desert sun burn me to a cinder!"

"You never could starve," said big Parker. "You've got enough fat between your skin and your bones to keep you going like a camel for a month! Besides, Pedrillo, your skin is so wonderfully thick that the sun never could burn through it. So have no fear!"

"Ah, fear eats me," said Pedrillo, smiting his hand against his stomach with force. "Fear eats me like a wolf! I lie in the shadow of this danger. We never should have begun this trail!"

"Now, Pedrillo," said Robert, "tell me honestly that you have missed the trail and that for the last three hours you have been riding blindly. Certainly I haven't seen a sign or a ghost of a sign. Have you, Dan?"

"Not a trace. Confess, Pedrillo!"

"I am aiming," said Pedrillo, "at those two gullies that open in the hills, yonder."

"Aiming at both of them?"

"Yes, because in one of them we'll pick up the trail again."

"Are you sure?"

"Alas, señor, I am more than sure. For I know that the men we are following do not want us to miss the trail!"

"What the devil are you talking about?" exclaimed Parker. "This is rank nonsense, Pedrillo!"

"Señor, it is true nevertheless."

"Tell us what makes you think so."

"Because these people we are following know how to make a trail problem, but the ones that they have left for us are so simple that a child could solve them."

"Are we children, Fernald and I?" asked the big foreman, frowning again.

"No, no, señor. Not in all things."

Pedrillo grinned again. He was as fond as a woman of making his point.

"One can never corner the scoundrel," admitted the big man. "But go on, Pedrillo. You haven't explained enough."

"It is this way, señor. They do just enough to make most

people think that they are trying to cover their trail. But I know that they could be cleverer if they wished."

"Well, Pedrillo, for three hours, as you admit, we've had not a ghost of a trail to follow. Explain that."

"Easily. Their trail this morning pointed for those same valleys in the foothills. They knew that if we lost the sign, we would cast ahead toward the hills."

"We'll see," murmured Parker. "I think this is nonsense."

"Nonsense, perhaps," said Fernald, as they resumed their journey, "but I'll tell you, Dan, that the Mexican is seldom wrong when he makes up his mind in earnest!"

"Perhaps so. Well, I still have the privilege of doubting. We'll get a better idea when we come into those gullies."

They came into the first of the passes between the hills in the late afternoon. There was no trace of the six horses; but the Mexican did not delay for a long search. It would be the other valley up which the six had gone. "And depend upon it, my friends, that we shall find the sign immediately we enter."

As he suggested, so it happened. They found the complete trail written at large in the crossing of a clay bank. Parker and Fernald stared at one another.

"But," said Parker, "of course they had to get up this gulch and they couldn't avoid this bank!"

"Yes," nodded the Mexican. "There is that loose sand on the other side which would hold a trail no better than water."

"Their horses were too tired to ride them through loose sand."

"Señor, a frightened man is never too tired to make himself safe!"

"Tell me, Pedrillo," said Robert in some heat, "what makes you think this? And what could be in the head of Señor Brennan?"

"It is very simple. A child could understand," said the

171

Mexican. "He is drawing us after him into the heart of the mountains, and there he will suddenly draw us into a trap. Look up yonder. Somewhere behind the cactus, one of his men is lying now with a glass trained on us, studying everything that we do."

Fernald and Parker looked up instinctively.

"That is an old trail," said Parker with decision. "They're still a great distance ahead of us."

"That trail, señor, was made no longer ago than noon."

"What is your reason for that?"

"This is a moist clay bank; the hoofprints are dry in the center, but still moist in the hollows on each side. If the horses had passed this way yesterday, the whole print would be dry now; if they had passed only within an hour, the whole print would be dark and moist."

"I've wondered how you could follow such long trails in the past," said he. "But now it's explained. You carry a hunting hound with you. I think that he's right, and Brennan may be holding a trap for us. We'll have to ride rifle in hand, old fellow!"

Robert shook his head.

"We have Oñate still with us," said he. "And one can trust him. He can scent danger as far as a wild horse. And if there's the least danger ahead of us, you can depend on him to smell it out!"

"Very well," said Parker. "But now comes the crux. I think we'll be dead men—or famous—inside of the next twenty-four hours, Bob. What do you say?"

Fernald said nothing. He had grown pale, his lips were a trifle compressed, and he looked forward up the valley with a peculiar eagerness. Dan Parker studied him with interest that was seasoned by a peculiar fear. For what would have been panic in another man, in Robert Fernald was the sudden and fierce working of the desire to kill. Parker watched, therefore, with a species of awe and wonder. But they did not speak to one another for some time. Though

172

the day was wearing late and the sun was low in the west, it shone down the length of that shallow valley and turned it into a meager trough of fire which turned the sweat on the horses to white salt, and seared the very eyelids of the riders.

The Mexican, in the meantime, rode his mule nervously, in an irregular line which waved back and forth from side to side of the ravine as he went from one vantage point to another.

"Look!" said Parker, "the impertinent scoundrels have brought their captives almost straight back to Larkin Valley!"

He had hardly finished speaking when Oñate came flying back to them, bowed over his saddle horn to make the better speed.

"Turn back, friends!" he gasped at them, as he went flying past with gray, pulpy face. "They are all there on the farther side of the hill!"

"Come back!" called Fernald harshly. The Mexican spurred his weary mule only the more vigorously.

"Come back, Oñate, or I'll shoot you out of the saddle!"

And Robert actually whipped his long rifle out of the scabbard which ran down the side of his saddle beneath his right knee.

"Good heavens, man, will you kill even Pedrillo?" exclaimed Dan Parker.

But Pedrillo was taking no chances with death. He glanced over his shoulder at the danger from the rear and instantly reined up and came back to them slowly, shaking his head in violent protest.

"They are all there on the farther side of the hill. They are all there, señor! Four devils, at least, and maybe more."

"The ladies, Pedrillo. Did you see the two ladies, also?"

"I saw the bait they are using for their trap," said Pedrillo. "But they are not women! They are not women, I swear to you!"

"He's gone out of his head," said Parker sternly. "Bob, let's you and I press ahead and pay no more attention to this gibbering idiot!"

"Ah, ah, ah!" gasped Pedrillo. "Then you are in the plot also, Señor Parker! You are working for Brennan! You are in the plot also!"

"You yellow-faced devil!" snarled big Parker and reached for the fat throat of Oñate; and found it, sinking the fingers deep in the rolling fat, until Oñate's tongue thrust out, and his eyes rolled up to heaven.

"Don't hurt him," said Fernald, without heat but in the manner of one who must be obeyed instantly.

Parker obediently released the Mexican.

"He needs to be flayed alive, Bob," he commented. "Did you hear? He said that I was—by heaven, I *shall* beat him to a pulp!"

He made another pass, but Pedrillo sought refuge behind his master. All the while his tongue was busy.

"Beware, señor. Think only a little moment!" he warned. "Is Señor Parker a fool?"

"Of course not. Does it follow that he's a villain, Pedrillo?"

"He is not a fool, you admit. Then he knows that he is not a great fighting man. Does he not? He is no Robert Fernald; he is no Brennan; and he is not even so good a fighter as any of those wild young men who live with Brennan. Is not that true?"

"Are you going to listen to any more of this sort of stuff?" asked Parker, raging with impatient anger.

"Let him talk himself out," replied Fernald. "I've learned before that words won't stay bottled up in him, and the easiest way is to let him turn the bottle upside down at once, even if it takes quite a time. For sooner or later I'll have to listen to every one of these words!"

"Not if he was gagged with a rope!" said Parker savagely.

174

"Listen! He is afraid! He would like to kill me!" said the Mexican. "He would like to hang me up. Because he fears lest I should make you believe in the truth! That is the way with him!"

So said Pedrillo, bellowing with surety. He was hot with conviction.

"Consider, señor," he went on, "that this same man, who is not a fool, was willing to ride off with you and a one-armed Mexican who cannot use weapons on the trail of the terrible Brennan. He did not ask any questions. He did not wonder what would happen when he met Brennan. He only said that he wanted to rush ahead to the fight. Tell me, then, if he is not a fool, why does he wish to throw his life away so soon?"

"Ah, Pedrillo," said Robert sadly, "you never could understand such a man as my friend Dan Parker. You cannot understand, therefore, why Dan Parker would risk his life on this trail to catch Brennan and his gang of devils!"

"I? I understand everything!" shouted Pedrillo, infuriated at this aspersion upon his faith and his stoutness of heart. "I'll die ten times a day for my little father. But he—he's a paid man! He's a hired hand on a ranch. And you tell me that he is going to commit suicide for the sake of the señorita who employs him? Bah, he is only a—"

The hard fist of Dan Parker shot straight for the chin of the Mexican, who dodged behind Robert Fernald, and the driving arm of Parker staggered the smaller man.

Fernald frowned a little, but then shrugged his shoulders.

"Let Pedrillo alone," said he. "And you, Oñate, don't be such a madman. You say that you have just seen the whole party of Brennan, and the two ladies among them—and yet they are not women after all! Is that sense, my friend?"

"I saw them ride. I saw the way that they sat the saddle! I know that they are men, señor!"

175

Fernald considered Pedrillo more seriously.

"He actually has seen something," reflected Fernald. "He has some sort of reason working in him, Dan."

"The scoundrel is frightened to death," said Dan Parker. "But I don't care what he's thinking, because I'm going to ride over the brow of that hill; and if Brennan and his gang are below, I'm going to shoot as I ride. Fernald, come with me or else stay here. I have my work cut out for me!"

With that, he swung the head of his horse away, and jogged briskly up the valley toward the rise of land beyond which, according to the Mexican, were Brennan's men and the women, or what seemed women, that he escorted.

Robert would have followed at once had it not been that the Mexican suddenly grasped his bridle reins and fell on his knees under the nose of Pinto.

"If you go, you are a dead man—beyond that ridge lies death or a terrible betrayal!" cried Oñate.

Robert looked down into a face that was convulsed with emotion.

"Pedrillo," said Robert kindly, "I believe that you have my interests at heart. I know that you wish what is best for me—"

"Alas, señor," said Pedrillo, beginning to weep, "I love you like a father, and like a son. I have been an evil man. I have done much wickedness. I have lied to you terribly. But now believe me. Do not ride over that ridge!"

"Take your hand from my reins," said Robert Fernald a little sternly. "I believe that you love me, Pedrillo. But I tell you, if there were ten thousand fighting men on the other side of that rise I would have to go with Parker against them!"

Pedrillo released the reins. He fell face down in the sands, sobbing heavily, so that his whole great body shook and trembled like marsh land underfoot.

Robert gave him a final glance, shook his head as though banishing from his mind any last indecision, and galloped

Pinto swiftly after Parker, who was now riding up the slope beyond.

After him came the voice of Pedrillo, thick, choked with sobs: "Señor Parker is a traitor! A traitor! Name of heaven, do not go with him!" But Robert closed his ears to the warning voice.

He saw Parker, a few lengths before him, drive over the crest; he heard the shout of the foreman; and then the rapid explosions from the rifle of the big fellow as he charged down the other slope. Then Pinto flicked over the summit, and in the hollow Robert saw a band of four men, and two figures of women, one sitting in a side saddle.

The next instant, guns spoke from the hollow, and big Dan Parker reeled heavily in the saddle, and fell forward, clutching blindly at the pommel of his saddle!

34

When Robert Fernald saw this happen, he knew that Parker was gone, so far as that fight was concerned; and Parker being gone, Robert gave himself up for dead. Had there been two or three men in that hollow—even such great fighters as Brennan and his gang—he would have felt that there was a ghost of a chance; but when he looked down, he saw the four ready, alert, guns in hand, and he knew that he could not crush them all.

He did not turn back, or waver for an instant. But suddenly he saw the sublime logic in this event. For the whole last part of his life, he had been pointing straight toward this instant. For had he not been roving here and there, searching out the great adventure, matching himself with impossible deeds? Now had come the deed which truly was impossible. He must fail, but he would fail gloriously, with a smoking gun in either hand.

He was about to straighten Pinto at the enemy when he heard a wild wailing cry behind him, and, looking over his shoulder for an instant, he had sight of the strangest picture, perhaps, that ever dawned upon human sight; and that was of the Mexican, charging over the brow of the hill to do battle with his master, and yelling as he came: "Halt, señor! In the name of heaven, let me die beside you!"

Fernald, amazed and staggered, shouted back to Pedrillo to save himself, and then turned Pinto toward the men in the hollow.

Three of them waited for him there, and now he saw that the seeming ladies had sprung down from their horses and thrown off their trailing mantles. They were men! A sort of masked battery, now ready to be turned upon Fernald in case of need.

Six to one! The thing became almost ridiculous. But Robert did not hesitate! How could he, being what he was, when he saw one figure detach itself from the rest and come straight out to meet him?

Yes, there was the magnificent form of Brennan riding toward him. The gun fighter had cast his hat aside, and his long gray hair blew back from his face as he came forward at a gentle canter. Brennan! What a vast lifting of the soul there was in Robert at that moment! Now, at least, he would be sure of destroying one of the band, and the most important of all! Brennan must go down before him! He laughed with a fierce joy; and Brennan, riding forth to meet this enemy, saw the laughter of grim ecstasy.

Yet Brennan did not turn back, and he did not swerve! Instead, he brought his pony to a halt and jerked the rifle to his shoulder.

"High and to the right!" said Robert, looking at the level

of the weapon. As though his words had directed the bullet, it flew above his head and to the side. The rifle spoke again—and the bullet hummed closer to the head of Fernald.

Then he fired in turn. He was at rather long range, but he had no thought of missing. Carelessly, half-blindly, as a good pistol shot will do, he snapped his gun into place and fired. And then he opened his eyes with amazement.

Brennan had not fallen!

No, there he sat in his saddle, the wind ruffling his long hair into waves of silver, his rifle poised for the third shot.

Yes, and he was smiling!

The very bottom of the world fell out, for Robert. He had missed! Missed utterly—and the target was a man and a horse! As fast as he could pull trigger, he showered five bullets from alternate guns.

Behold, there sat Brennan upon his horse, his rifle still poised for the finishing shot—and every one of Robert's bullets had failed of its mark!

A sort of hysterical cold came upon Robert Fernald, then. He was closing upon the outlaw with the last fury of Pinto's rush.

He cast aside the guns which had failed him. He drew the long hunting knife from his belt, and he waved it above his head with a shout.

A change came in the face of Brennan; the smile went out; the gun spoke loudly. And poor Pinto pitched down head foremost in death.

Over his head he flung his rider. Robert saw a blue flash of heaven lit blindingly by the westering sun, and then all light went out.

And as the darkness rushed across his senses, he heard the scream of the Mexican far behind him as the other guns spoke.

Had Pedrillo gone down, too?

Yes, and in exactly the same fashion. The rifle of Brennan

179

had spoken at the proper moment as he saw Oñate plunging down the slope at him. A wild picture! For Oñate had seized the reins in his teeth, and so left his arm free to grasp his revolver. He came on, shooting blindly, foolishly. The steady rifle of Brennan was tipped up; it spoke; and the mule rolled in death, and cast Pedrillo far ahead, and laid him senseless.

So here were two of the three assailants helpless upon the ground.

Brennan's men rushed eagerly around them. Oñate had a leg twisted under him, unquestionably broken and broken badly! But Robert Fernald lay face up, with a bloody gash upon his brow. No, he was merely stunned, unless there were internal injuries.

What of Dan Parker? It was a most amazing thing to see him ride straight in on the Brennan band, and when he was among them stop his horse and drop to his feet—then sink upon a rock.

"In the name of heaven, are they both dead?" cried Parker, white of face.

Brennan himself came back to Parker.

"They're not dead," he declared. "They'll come around in time, but they're out for a few minutes. Old boy, you played a good part there! But even at that, I thought I was going to be a gone goose at the last minute. Look here!"

He pointed to the hunting knife of Fernald, sticking deep in his saddle.

"He threw it as his horse fell," said Brennan. "I thought I was gone when I seen that streak of silver! And every shot that he fired was a bull's-eye, Dan. He sprinkled me with lead dust every time. Look here!"

He pointed to his shirt; it was flecked with dots of black.

"What did you put in those slugs, Dan?" he asked.

"It was a hunch that I got a long time ago," grinned Parker. "It's lead, you see. Real lead. But it's only crystals that are packed in under an outer film. It looks smooth and hard, and it weighs like lead. But when you fire, it scatters like dust in the air. Now, for heaven's sake get his fallen guns and his cartridge belt and load them with real bullets, will you? Since I put in the phony ones at our camp, last night, I've been in a stew."

"Afraid that he'd take a crack at something along the way?" Brennan nodded understandingly.

"Yes, and find out that there was something wrong with the ammunition, you understand?"

"Chuck," said Brennan, "get the belt off Fernald and line it with new bullets. Same number that there are in it. Shake the cartridges out of his guns, too, and put in real ones. We'd have nothing but wasted work if he was ever to find out! And here, Sam, help to get a bandage around Parker's head, will you? Prick your finger and get some blood on it. It's got to look as though you were grazed by a bullet and knocked silly that way, Dan!"

Four of the men were working over the fallen warriors, and now they could hear the loud groaning of the Mexican up the slope, though still he was unconscious.

In the meantime, the bandage was wrapped around the head of Parker. His gun belt was taken away, and his hands were tied before him.

"Will it do any good, though?" said Parker. "Ain't he going to find out?"

"If he finds out," said Brennan, with a shudder, "God help us! I was a dead man six times, Dan. I never seen such shooting from the back of a running horse! Six times he dusted me! And when I seen him coming like a madman— the first two bullets I fired to kill—and missed. Then I seen that you'd done your work right, when he opened fire. So I waited, and let the poor horse have it at the last jump. If it's possible to break the nerve of any man, Dan, this ought to keep Fernald from wearing guns again. But—I have my doubts! He's a wildcat! He ain't human!"

"And if he should ever guess!" said Parker with a groan.

"If he ever should guess that this was a put-up job! Why, the Mexican had a hunch at the last minute and I thought that I was a gone goose. Would have been, except that Fernald never suspects any one whom he calls a friend."

"A hard job," sighed Brennan. "I wish that I'd never started it. But who could resist, with a girl like her cryin' and beggin' for my help! She loves him, Dan, the way that few men ever have been loved."

"Aye," said Parker, "and besides, she's paying big! What did you do with the pair of them?"

"Just as we planned. They shifted from their horses at the point where Chuck and Sam met us. Took their horses and headed for Larkin Valley. And there they're waiting for news. I'll send in a boy with the good word—if you can call it good!"

35

No hint of these happenings came to Robert, of course, as he lay senseless. And when he recovered and opened his eyes, he saw nothing to betray the plot which had revolved so cunningly around him. What he observed was Dan Parker, his hands bound together before him, his head encircled by a blood-stained bandage; and then, as he sat up, Robert heard the terrible groaning of Pedrillo Oñate, who, in turn, had recovered his senses, urged on by an incessant spur of sharp pain.

Brennan in person was at work over the Mexican. Men said that, in early days, the lone rider had been a doctor. At least, it was certain that he knew much of the ways of a healer. And now he was putting his art to a practical use, as he incased the broken leg of the Mexican in rudely improvised splints. A great dram of brandy gave Pedrillo force to endure his present pain. His groans diminished. Now Robert, his own hands tied in front of him, was permitted to go to poor Oñate and sit beside him.

A flash of joy struck across the face of the Mexican. His eyes glittered with happiness. "They told me that you were alive, señor," said he. "But I thought that the devils were lying. Glorious Virgin of Guadalupe! It is because I vowed six tall candlesticks of pure beeswax. She saved you! She turned the bullets from you and made them strike Pinto! Señor, little father, let me have your hand and feel that it is yourself, and not a ghost that is here and—Hai! Hellfire take them! They are killing me! Stop them, little father!"

He clung to the hand of Robert, and remained clinging to it until the operation was finished. Then another dram of brandy, combined with the exhaustion of great pain and the aftereffects of a shock of nervous excitement, washed Pedrillo deep into a gulf of sleep.

Brennan, stiff-lipped and stern from the surgical work which he had been doing, stood back from the Mexican and looked to Robert Fernald with a faint smile.

"How did you manage it, Fernald?" asked he. "What medicine did you use to turn this great hulk of a coward into a hero today?"

Presently they prepared to march. A litter was made for Pedrillo and slung between two horses, then the party journeyed on up the valley, turned sharply into a little twisting ravine, and, where the stream spread in a small pool, they made their camp.

Robert was with Pedrillo, who was coming back to his senses again with deep groans and occasional loud yells of pain.

"Patience, señor!" said the Mexican. "We shall have them yet. If they cannot be trailed to this place, all the men in the desert are blind as bats. Patience, señor. A moment's patience is a ten years' comfort, and he that can be patient finds his foe at his feet. They will trail us here and bag all the villains, señor!"

Robert could not reply except to say: "Be quiet, Pedrillo. Keep your strength. You have been through a great deal. Now save yourself. God knows how long it will be before you can be moved from this place to the care of a good doctor."

"Señor," said the Mexican, "you give me foolish advice and worse comfort. God defend me from all doctors, I say first of all. When the doctor comes in at one door, death comes in by another. Death is the shadow of the doctor, señor. And it is by death that the doctor lives! No, God defend me from doctors, I say! And above all, do not tell me to be silent. If it is not for the music of my own tongue, I shall go mad thinking of the pain in which I lie here."

In this manner Pedrillo talked, twisting himself to and fro, and never resting until Robert had propped up his head a little. He rolled a cigarette for Oñate, and the latter smoked it with great sighs of relief. But still he talked, making the smoke bubble and break at his lips. He talked, indeed, until he seemed quite to forget his pain from the broken leg.

"He doesn't need an opiate," said Brennan, pausing to listen. "Not so long as he can keep hinges on his tongue!"

When Pedrillo at last fell asleep again, Robert had a chance to talk with Parker. The two were left quite alone, and allowed to talk freely and secretly with one another. With his bound hands, Robert took the imprisoned ones of Parker and pressed them hard.

"Old fellow," said Fernald, "I've seen a good many brave things done. But I've never seen anything finer than the way you drove over the top of that hill. Only, tell me this, why did you do it? Why didn't you wait for me? Then we could have made the charge together and perhaps—God knows!—we might have done something, working together!"

Parker frowned at the ground and then peered at the dusky sky, for it was long after the sunset.

"It was Pedrillo," said he, speaking rapidly and in a mumbling voice. "It was Pedrillo. I had to do something to show you—"

Here he stuck, and frowned again at the ground.

"Tush!" said Robert. "As though I could have doubted you! As though I could have doubted you for a second! But—what do you think Brennan will do with us?"

"God knows," said Parker. "It seems that his main idea, after the ladies gave him the slip in the middle of the desert and after he found that we were following, was to trap you and fight with you hand to hand."

Dan managed to raise his head and look Robert in the eye. But Robert was staring gloomily into the distance.

"He wanted to beat you," went on Parker, "and—"

"And he did it," said Robert sadly. "But now, what?"

"I think he's holding you in the hope that if he could not keep Miss Larkin for ransom, at least he may be able to make her ransom you!"

Robert shook his head.

"Why not?" asked Parker. "We've both done something for her. And she has money enough to help us!"

"It would do me no good," said Robert. "I've been thinking the thing out, you see."

"Thinking to what end?" asked Parker, his voice turning very sharp.

"For you, yes. The ransom would be all very well for you, Dan. Of course you should get your freedom. But it's a different matter with me."

"I don't see that."

"It's this way. I never could live happily, remembering how I stood up to one man, and was beaten like that!"

"Do you mean it?"

"Yes. I mean that I have to have another chance at Brennan. Now, or later."

"Another chance?" cried Parker. "But, old fellow, don't you see how it is? He met you fairly and squarely. He beat you, certainly. You can't expect to be the best man in the world, you know."

"I understand that he's the better man," said Robert, falling back into his gloomy thought. "And I'd rather be a dead man than a living man with that thought. He beat me fairly and squarely, as you say. And I wish that the bullet had killed me instead of dropping poor Pinto. That was a brave little cayuse, Dan!"

He sighed.

"You mean," interpreted Parker, "that if you're ransomed here, you'll keep on the trail of Brennan until you have a chance to fight the thing out with him again?"

"Of course," answered Robert. "There's nothing else for me to do, really!"

Parker said no more. He fell into a brown study, and his reflections did not seem to be very pleasant ones. In the meantime a camp fire had been lighted. Brennan and another came back from a brief hunting tour of the ravine loaded with rabbits for the evening meal. And in the few short moments the odor of roasted meat was drifting across the air.

The stars came out, the dim and distant desert stars. The hungry men were so silent that, now and again, one could hear the horses grinding their forage in the darkness. The fire crackled merrily. Never had there been a scene of greater peace. But for two there was no beauty in the scene—to Robert, seated on a fallen log and staring at the stars with sightless eyes of thought; to Parker, who hunted out Brennan for a private conference.

Brennan, for his part, seemed in the best of spirits. After all, he had undertaken a most delicate and ticklish business and had brought it through to an apparently triumphant issue with the secret help of Dan Parker. Therefore, he was whistling softly as he took his share of roasted rabbit to one side and sat down to eat. There Parker joined him. He sat in silence, regardless of the share of food which had been given to him.

"Hello," said Brennan, "is there sand in that meat, Dan?"

"Damn the meat!" said Parker.

"What's wrong?"

"Guess, then."

"You mean the kid? Why, he seems to be pretty well in hand. He ain't said a word, hardly. What's your drift, Dan?"

"Why," explained Parker, "what's the main job, here?"

"To bust the spirit of the kid and show him that he ain't almighty with a gun. What else?"

"Nothin' else," said Parker. "That's exactly the main job. To sort of gentle him down, so he'll be willing to retire to Larkin Ranch and marry the finest girl in the world and settle down with her. That's the main job."

"It's done," said Brennan with decision. "He's had his lesson."

"Old son," said Parker, "he's just after telling me that he'll never live happy until he's had a chance to fight the thing out with you again!"

"Fury and fire!" breathed Brennan. "Do you mean that?"

"I mean that. Now, how will it be for you, Tiger, to stand up to that kid again?"

"I'll see him hanged first!" said Brennan without the slightest hesitation. "He dusted me with six bullets running. I was a dead man six times over before I managed to bring down his horse. No, no, Dan! I take my chance with any man, even old as I am; but I don't take any chances with a shooting machine like that kid! Missing a shot just ain't in his makeup!"

"Suppose he's ransomed? Then he immediately starts on your trail and sticks to it until he gets a chance to—"

187

"I'd simply have the boys lay for him and massacre him, Parker. Suicide ain't in my line."

Parker lighted a cigarette, and he sighed deeply.

"He's over there admiring you," explained Parker. "He's been telling me how much better a man you are than him. And at the same time, he couldn't live, y'understand, knowing that he's been beat, even when he was beat fair and square. But suppose, Tiger, just supposin', he should ever get wind of what really happened—or even should he find out that I really wasn't knocked silly by a bullet but that I was in the game on your side from the start—"

Tiger Brennan whistled.

Then he added: "We'll wait till we get word from Miss Larkin. Then we'll see. We'll see what's to happen!"

So they waited. And the messenger sent to the Larkin Ranch returned the next morning before noon with a letter for Brennan. The letter was brief, and amazingly to the point:

You've done wonderfully well. I hardly see how you managed it. I'm inclosing another check for five thousand. Just to show you how I appreciate the skill you've used. Get Fernald to the ranch as fast as you can. And, for heaven's sake, never let him guess how this has happened!

Then Brennan called Parker and young Robert Fernald before him.

"Boys," said he, "I'm mighty glad to say that Miss Larkin didn't waste no time. She's sent down the coin that I needed. And so the pair of you can go free. But you don't go free until you make a bargain with me. I've used you a bit rough, and no doubt you have a hankering to get even with me. Now, lads, I want your promise to me that you'll never take my trail and never pull a gun against me. I'll take your word for that, because you're a pair of honorable gents."

188

"Certainly!" said Parker. "I'm not fool enough to want any more of your game, Tiger. Here's my hand on it!"

"Thanks, Parker. Then you're free. Wait till I cut this rope. There you are!"

The rope fell instantly from the hands of Parker, and Brennan directed one of his men to restore the guns and belt to the liberated prisoner. Then he turned to young Fernald.

"The same deal goes with you, Fernald," he said kindly. "Just shake on this deal and—"

"I think you mean very well in this," said Fernald. "But the trouble is, Brennan, that I can't do it."

"And why not, then?"

"Because, sooner or later, I've got to get at you, Brennan. We've had one fight, and all the winning has gone to you. Perhaps you're a better man. But I want to stand up to you once more and finish the deal. Living is no good to me, with a better man just around the corner!"

Brennan strode close and towered above Robert's five feet and eight inches.

"Kid," cried he, "are you plain batty? Are you askin' me to blow you to hell? Because once there, I can't blow you back again!"

Fernald merely smiled. It seemed that this blustering only served to give him more strength of purpose.

"The sun is right over our heads," said he, "and so it can't shine in the eyes of either of us. Why not take this time, Brennan? Why not take this time and have it out? I'd as soon be buried here as anywhere!"

Brennan turned on his heel and strode away.

"You've made a fool of yourself," said Parker anxiously to Robert. "Let me call him back."

"Why did he quit me?" asked Robert, bewildered.

"Because he's not an idiot," said Parker, with a ready wit. "He's beaten you once, and let you live. Why should he risk himself against you a second time? He's a gold digger, not a gambler, Bob!"

Brennan, sitting apart, turned the matter back and forth in his mind. For a half hour or more he remained lost in his brooding. Then he rose with a grim face. He looked up and pointed to two or three small black spots in the sky.

"Let the buzzards finish this argument," he said. "I've offered this fellow his life; he won't have it on decent terms. Well, that's the end of him. Fernald, you're going to die here like a dog!"

Fernald stiffened a little.

"If you do it, Brennan," said he, "you'll be more detested than a mad dog through the range."

"I'll take my chance on that. Boys, stand him against that wall, will you? And give me that new Colt—"

"Wait a minute, chief," said big Charlie Dashwood, gray with disgust and fear. "D'you mean that you're going to butcher him like—like a pig?"

"And what have you to say to that?" roared Brennan; but as he whirled on Dashwood, he winked, a broad and solemn wink, seen not only by Charlie but by the rest of the band.

"All right," said Dashwood, frowning to keep from smiling. "I'll stand him up for you. Bandage his eyes?"

"No, no!" said Robert. "You needn't fear that I'll dodge. And—I want to see it coming!"

He himself stepped back against the appointed wall.

Brennan cursed softly. And then: "Hold on," he cried. "It ain't right that the master should go before the man. Bring out the Mexican and prop him up against the wall!"

It was done. But when poor Oñate saw what was contemplated he screamed like a woman.

"Señor Brennan, noble and kind señor, I'll be your slave. I never will betray you! I'll be truer to you than to Señor Fernald. Bah! What is he to me? What is he compared with a great man like you, señor! But do not kill me! Oh, my

God! I have a mother—and an old father—I have seven children to starve without me—I am—"

"A pair of you hold him up by each shoulder," said the cruel Brennan.

"Señor Brennan, I swear that I shall give you my solemn honor!"

"Bah!" said Brennan. "You have no honor. Hold him up, boys, and I'll soon have this over—"

He balanced the revolver in his hand. Oñate was supported on either side, so that his breast was open to the bullet.

"One moment," said Oñate with a changed voice. "I defy you and spit in your face, dog of a pirate and cutthroat. Señor Fernald, little father, pity me and forgive me! I denied you because I loved life. But if God gave me the right to die for you and so set you free, I should go to my death smiling. Tell me that you believe me, little father!"

"Ready!" said Brennan. "Say your last prayer, if you've got one to say!"

"Señor," said Oñate to Fernald, overlooking the threat of the ready gun, "we meet in heaven. It is only one moment of pain. Adios, amigo!"

"Brennan!" shouted Fernald.

Brennan stepped back a little, and scowled at his prisoner.

"Don't fire on him," gasped Robert Fernald. "I'll give you my word—I'll do whatever you want!"

36

So, by the wit and cruel imagination of Tiger Brennan, Fernald was tamed and his career as a slayer of men was brought to an end. For these were the terms imposed on him by Brennan: Never to seek the society of a dangerous man; never to respond to a challenge to fight; never to draw a weapon, except in the actual defense of his life.

So Robert submitted. And an odd document was drawn up by the hand of Brennan, stating in exact terms what was to be done. "Because," said Brennan, "your memory might fail you one of these days, but I'll keep a copy, and you'll keep the other. And there you are!"

How did it happen that Brennan was willing to trust merely to the pledged word of this man who was a stranger to him? Well, Robert was not really a stranger to any one in the West. All men had heard of his exploits, and all men knew a good deal about his work with guns and men; above all, he was famous for an unstained honor which never yet had broken faith upon great matters or upon small. So Brennan was willing to trust.

Half an hour later, Tiger Brennan was gone with his men, disappearing in a whirlwind of dust up the ravine, and leaving Robert, the stricken Pedrillo, and Dan Parker without horses, without food, without so much as a hunting knife as means of helping themselves.

However, they did not have long in which to wonder what would come of them. Over the edge of the western hill they heard the rattling of hoofs, and there came down into the ravine half a dozen staunch riders, who were rec-

192

ognized afar by Parker as members of his own crew, workers on the Larkin Ranch. They greeted Parker with much noisy enthusiasm. They greeted Robert Fernald with an awed respect. And even to Pedrillo they showed a singular amount of attention.

They made a litter for him, the softest that could be fashioned, and started the trek across the hills, climbing up and up to the beautiful, cool meadow lands of the Larkin Ranch.

Robert and Dan Parker walked together behind the procession for a time, but Robert was terribly in the dumps, and he could not raise his head to talk. So Parker hurried on to the others. They left Robert trailing behind, breathing their dust, the most bedraggled and woebegone figure that one could imagine.

And, in the meantime, the party in the lead made merry, badgering Pedrillo.

"You scoundrel," a grinning cowpuncher would say, "tell me how come that you offered to let Brennan shoot you? D'you think that his bullets was made of paper, maybe?"

Pedrillo lay back in his bed of pine branches and puffed cigarettes and smiled upon them, for he was content with the world.

"Great things cannot be understood by little men," Pedrillo would say. "Pardon, señor, but you throw your shadow upon me!"

So they laughed and tormented one another. But Pedrillo knew that he had left the ranks of the rogues and, against his own fondest expectations, established himself among the ranks of honest men. It made him feel very dizzy; but it made him feel that God was very great, being able to accomplish even such a miracle as this!

So the caravan came in sight of the house, where a solitary rider swept toward them—beautiful Beatrice Larkin, her face drawn and her eyes brilliant.

"But where's the man you went to get?" she asked,

cruelly overlooking Parker and poor Pedrillo. "Where's Bobbie Fernald? Where's he?"

He had disappeared.

"I'll get him in five minutes!" said Parker, turning pale. "He was with us, I'd swear, not long ago—he must be back beyond that stretch of hummocks."

She cast one terrible and blasting glance upon him, and then her horse darted away; and the others rushed off, also, scattering here and there in a wild search.

But it was Beatrice who found him—far back—five miles back—in the center of a little circle of poplars that stood around a spring. There he was, sitting beside the pool, his face in his hands.

And when she rushed her horse through the trees and cried out at the sight of him, he did not raise his head.

She flung herself out of the saddle and ran to him.

"Bobbie, Bobbie! I thought you were lost!"

"I am," said he, and stood before her. "I'm lost, Beatrice, shamed, disgraced, and done for. No man will ever want me for a friend again!"

"And the women, Bobbie?" she asked.

"No proud woman ever would want me in her house as a friend," said he.

"Perhaps not; but as a husband, Bobbie—that would be a rather different thing."

"You're making a joke of me, Beatrice," said Robert, with a sad dignity.

"Only half, Bobbie," said she.

Certainly she never stopped laughing at him, even when he was the father of her children; and certainly even the cowpunchers on the place used to smile as he went by; for to the end he remained rather a shrinking figure. And one hardly could have said whether or not he was a happy man. At least in many a way he was never truly content. There were only two people in the world who could make him laugh.

194

One was his wife.

The other was Pedrillo, who never left that valley so long as he lived.

There is another matter which must be mentioned. Burgess failed to harm McCoy; and Burgess himself was killed by the kick of a powerful little mule.

As for the enormous hoax of the pretended kidnaping of Beatrice Larkin and her aunt, rumors about it flew everywhere; certainly big Brennan never was accused of it as of a crime, but as of a joke; but no convincing tale of the truth ever came to the ears of Robert Fernald. He had passed into a mildly happy dream. But still his eyes were fixed on the wild heights of life, and he despised the quiet ways in which he found himself.